CW00468470

Nightmares Before Bedtime
(Short Horror Stories Collection)

Tim O'Rourke

First Edition Published by Ravenwoodgreys

Copyright 2023 by Tim O'Rourke

More books by Tim O'Rourke

Kiera Hudson Series One
Vampire Shift (Kiera Hudson Series 1) Book 1
Vampire Wake (Kiera Hudson Series 1) Book 2
Vampire Hunt (Kiera Hudson Series 1) Book 3
Vampire Breed (Kiera Hudson Series 1) Book 4
Wolf House (Kiera Hudson Series 1) Book 5
Vampire Hollows (Kiera Hudson Series 1) Book 6
Kiera Hudson Series Two
Dead Flesh (Kiera Hudson Series 2) Book 1
Dead Night (Kiera Hudson Series 2) Book 2
Dead Angels (Kiera Hudson Series 2) Book 3
Dead Statues (Kiera Hudson Series 2) Book 4
Dead Seth (Kiera Hudson Series 2) Book 5
Dead Wolf (Kiera Hudson Series 2) Book 6
Dead Water (Kiera Hudson Series 2) Book 7
Dead Push (Kiera Hudson Series 2) Book 8
Dead Lost (Kiera Hudson Series 2) Book 9
Dead End (Kiera Hudson Series 2) Book 10
Kiera Hudson Series Three
*The Creeping Men (Kiera Hudson Series Three)
Book 1*
*The Lethal Infected (Kiera Hudson Series Three)
Book 2*
*The Adoring Artist (Kiera Hudson Series Three)
Book 3*

Silent Night (Book 6)

Kiera Hudson: The Victorian Adventures

The Victorian Adventures (Part 1)
The Victorian Adventures (Part 2)
The Victorian Adventures (Part 3)
The Victorian Adventures (Part 4)
The Victorian Adventures (Part 5)
The Victorian Adventures (Part 6)
The Victorian Adventures (Part 7)

Kiera Hudson: Love, Blood & Vampires

Kiera Hudson 1988 (Part One)
Kiera Hudson 1988 (Part Two)

Werewolves of Shade

Werewolves of Shade (Part One)
Werewolves of Shade (Part Two)
Werewolves of Shade (Part Three)
Werewolves of Shade (Part Four)
Werewolves of Shade (Part Five)
Werewolves of Shade (Part Six)

Vampires of Maze

Vampires of Maze (Part One)
Vampires of Maze (Part Two)
Vampires of Maze (Part Three)
Vampires of Maze (Part Four)
Vampires of Maze (Part Five)
Vampires of Maze (Part Six)

Witches of Twisted Den

Witches of Twisted Den (Part One)
Witches of Twisted Den (Part Two)

Witches of Twisted Den (Part Three)
Witches of Twisted Den (Part Four)
Witches of Twisted Den (Part Five)
Witches of Twisted Den (Part Six)

Cowgirl & Creature

Cowgirl & Creature (Book One)
Cowgirl & Creature (Book Two)
Cowgirl & Creature (Book Three)
Cowgirl & Creature (Book Four)
Cowgirl & Creature (Book Five)
Cowgirl & Creature (Book Six)
Cowgirl & Creature (Book Seven)
Cowgirl & Creature (Book Eight)

The Mirror Realm (The Lacey Swift Series)

The Mirror Realm (Book One)
The Mirror Realm (Book Two)
The Mirror Realm (Book Three)
The Mirror Realm (Book Four)

Moon Trilogy

Moonlight (Moon Trilogy) Book 1
Moonbeam (Moon Trilogy) Book 2
Moonshine (Moon Trilogy) Book 3

The Clockwork Immortals

Stranger (Part One)
Stranger (Part Two)
Stranger (Part Three)

The Jack Seth Novellas

Hollow Pit (Book One)

Black Hill Farm (Books 1 & 2)

Black Hill Farm (Book 1)
Black Hill Farm: Andy's Diary (Book 2)
Sydney Hart Novels
Witch (A Sydney Hart Novel) Book 1
Yellow (A Sydney Hart Novel) Book 2
Raven (A Sydney Hart Novel (Book 3)
The Tessa Dark Trilogy
Stilts (Book 1)
Zip (Book 2)
Sink (Book 3)
The Mechanic
The Mechanic
The Dark Side of Nightfall Trilogy
The Dark Side of Nightfall (Book One)
The Dark Side of Nightfall (Book Two)
The Dark Side of Nightfall (Book Three)
Samantha Carter Series
Vampire Seeker (Book One)
Vampire Flappers (Book Two)
Vampire Watchmen (Book Three)
Vampire Knight (A Reimagining of Vampire Shift)
Vampire Knight
The Charley Shepard
Saving the Dead
Nightmares Before Bedtime
The Underground Ripper
Dead In The Basement
Dead Doll

The Underground Ripper

For Lynda O'Rourke

Chapter One

Colin's fingers trembled as he picked up the latest edition of the evening newspaper. The headline screamed, *Underground Ripper Strikes Again!* He furtively licked his lips, his heart pounding with a mixture of fear and excitement. Colin liked to keep his own company, shunning friends, and even his colleagues at the local bar where he was employed as a pot washer. To those that passed Colin on the street, he was an unassuming twenty-one year-old man, with mousy brown hair and glasses that were held together with tape. His forehead, cheeks and chin blazed red with what looked like adolescent acne, despite his age. But beneath his ordinary— sometimes awkward—appearance, an obsession festered.

"Another one," he whispered, eyes

devouring the grisly details of the latest murder on the London Underground.

His pulse quickened as he imagined the scene, the blood, and the fear in the victim's eyes. It was a fascination bordering on worship for the elusive killer known as the Underground Ripper.

"Let's see where you'll fit," Colin muttered excitedly to himself, scanning the walls of his cramped apartment. The small space was a shrine to the brutal murders that haunted the city. Newspaper clippings plastered every inch of the walls, their edges yellowing with age. Dates and locations scribbled in red ink connected them like a twisted spider's web. In the center hung a crudely drawn interpretation of the Ripper's face—a face that haunted Colin's dreams.

The apartment was dimly lit, casting long shadows over the threadbare furniture and sparse belongings. A single bed occupied one corner, its sheets tangled and tossed aside. Next to it stood a small table, littered with more news articles, pencils, and a well-thumbed notebook filled with meticulous notes about each murder. In another corner, a rickety chair faced the wall, allowing Colin the perfect vantage point to study his macabre collection.

"Ah, here we go," he said, carefully pinning the new article to the wall amongst the others, connecting the bloody dots. He stepped back to admire his handiwork, feeling a shiver of satisfaction run down his spine.

"Another masterpiece," he whispered, his hands feeling clammy with nervous excitement. "You're a legend, Ripper." His eyes darted from one article to another, consuming every gory detail as the darkness of the room closed in around him.

"Who will be next?" Colin wondered out loud, the question hanging heavy in the stale air.

The Underground Ripper's reign of terror had consumed him, and he couldn't help but crave more. But for now, he was content to stand in the dim light, surrounded by the echoes of death, and lose himself in the twisted world that had become his obsession.

Chapter Two

The blood, the screams—Colin could almost hear them as he read each gruesome detail in the newspaper articles pinned to his walls. He licked his lips, imagining the cold steel of the Ripper's knife slicing through warm flesh and the fear in his victims' eyes. The Underground Ripper had become a dark idol for him, a twisted figure to emulate. How exhilarating it would be to feel that same power coursing through his veins.

"Tonight," he whispered to himself, feeling a thrill race up his spine. "Tonight, I'll finally be like you."

Colin paced back and forth in his cramped apartment, the floorboards creaking under his weight. He felt restless, as if the very air around him was charged with electricity. His thoughts raced, devising the perfect plan to honor his murderous idol.

"Let's see…" he muttered, tapping a pencil

against his chin. "The Ripper always targets women traveling alone on the London Underground. Late at night, when there are fewer potential witnesses." He paused, picturing the dimly lit platform where he'd make his move. "I can do that. Just need to find the right victim."

His heart pounded in his chest as he considered the next step. "And the weapon...a knife. A long, sharp one, just like the Ripper's." Colin grinned, imagining the sensation of the blade piercing skin, the warmth of the blood spilling over his hands.

"Quick and brutal," he continued, excitement bubbling within him. "But not too quick. I want to savour it, just like you do, Ripper." He closed his eyes, envisioning the moment his victim would realise their fate.

"But how will I get away with it?" Colin scratched his pimple infested chin, brows furrowed in concentration. "The police have been hunting the Ripper for months, and they still haven't caught him. What's his secret?"

He thought for a moment, his eyes scanning the newspaper articles. Then it dawned on him—the Ripper always seemed to vanish into thin air after each murder. "He must know the tunnels like the back of his hand," Colin concluded. "That's how he escapes. I'll need to study them, find my own escape route."

With a newfound determination, he grabbed his notebook and began sketching out a map of the London Underground, marking potential hiding spots and escape routes. He would leave no stone unturned, no detail overlooked. Colin was certain that he could carry out his plan flawlessly, honouring the legacy of the Underground Ripper while evading capture.

"Tonight," he repeated, his voice low and sinister. "I will become you, Ripper. And they'll never catch me."

Chapter Three

The overhead fluorescent light cast a sickly glow over the deserted platform, bathing it in an unnatural glow. Colin's heart raced as he stepped onto the train, his boots echoing through the empty carriage. The scent of stale air and sweat hung heavy around him, but it did little to deter his focus.

"Patience," he whispered to himself, his breath fogging up the carriage window as he scanned the platform for any sign of a lone female traveller. "She'll come, just like the others did."

His fingers drummed impatiently against the cold metal handrail, the anticipation gnawing away at him. The train lurched forward, leaving the desolate station behind. He wandered through the carriages, his eyes darting to every corner and every seat, seeking out the target that continued to elude him.

"Where are you?" Colin muttered under his breath, frustration making his blood boil and skin itch. His thoughts were a tangled mess of bloodlust and desire, his obsession with the Underground Ripper driving him further toward the edge of insanity.

As the minutes dragged on, his irritation grew. Each stop provided nothing more than another empty platform, devoid of the prey he so desperately searched for. He clenched his fists, nails digging into his palms as he fought to maintain control.

"Damn it," he growled, slamming his fist against the nearest seat. "Why can't I find her? The Ripper always does." His mind reeled with images of the Ripper's mutilated victims, their bodies twisted and broken, a testament to the killer's skill and brutality.

Perhaps the Ripper is smarter than you think, a voice whispered in the back of his mind, taunting him. *Maybe he knows when and where to strike, while you fumble around, helplessly.*

"Shut up!" Colin snapped, his voice cracking as he tried to banish the intrusive thoughts. He couldn't bear the idea that he might not be as cunning or as ruthless as the Ripper. "I'll find her, just like he does. I'll prove it."

But with each passing station and no sign of a suitable victim, doubt began to seep in, poisoning his already warped mind. The nagging voice in his head continued to mock him, reminding him that perhaps he was no match for the legendary Underground Ripper after all.

"Maybe I'm not ready," Colin admitted to himself, his shoulders slumping in defeat. He leaned against the cold window of the carriage, his breath fogging up the glass once more as he stared out into the darkness of the tunnels. "But I will be. I have to be."

The train rattled on through the night, echoing the mounting frustration and desperation within Colin's tormented soul.

Chapter Four

As the train pulled out of the next station, Colin's eyes were drawn to a figure in the adjacent carriage. She must have boarded the train unnoticed by him and she now sat alone on a seat, her long dark hair cascading over her shoulders like a waterfall of shadows. The dim light from the overhead fixtures glinted off her pale skin and the silver crucifix that hung around her neck. Her clothes were simple, yet elegant— a black dress that clung to her slender frame, accentuating her curves. If she hadn't looked so damn hot, Colin could have mistaken her for a nun, what with her long black dress and the crucifix hung about her slender neck. A religious woman, perhaps?

"She'll be meeting her God sooner than she realises," Colin muttered to himself, a twisted grin spreading across his face.

His heart raced as he watched the young

woman through the window that separated the carriages. He could almost feel the chilling thrill of the knife in his hand, carving into her creamy, smooth flesh just as the Ripper had done with his other victims. Excitement filled him with a perverse sense of satisfaction, igniting a spark deep within him.

"Hello there, my lovely," he whispered to himself, over the clickety-clack of the train's motion as it raced through the underground tunnels far below London. "You have no idea what fate has in store for you tonight," he almost giggled to himself as he slowly got up out of his seat and made his way along the carriage as it lurched from side to side, racing at speed over ancient tracks.

Slowly and deliberately, Colin slid the door open between the carriages, stepping into the one occupied by his unsuspecting prey. His footfalls were soft, muffled by the sound of the mechanical workings of the train, as he made his way towards her. With every step, his excitement grew, mingling with the bloodlust racing through his veins.

"Easy now," he whispered to himself, a cautionary reminder to keep his composure. "Don't rush this. Savour it, just like the Ripper would. Take your time, enjoy the thrill of the kill."

His pulse quickened at the thought of his deranged idol, the Underground Ripper. The grisly scenes left behind by the enigmatic killer haunted Colin's dreams and fuelled his own twisted fantasies. Now, finally, he had found someone who could help him bring those fantasies to life.

"I can't even begin to imagine what he'll think when he hears about this?" Colin grinned insanely to himself, his eyes locked on the young woman as she glanced absently out of the carriage window at the passing tunnel walls. "He'll know that someone out there understands him, admires him even. And I...I will be the one to show him."

As he drew within touching distance—killing distance—of the young woman sitting at the end of the carriage oblivious to his murderous presence, Colin paused, taking a moment to steady himself before putting his perverse plan into action. He could feel the adrenaline flooding his system, his body trembling with anticipation and his cock stiffening with desire.

Here goes nothing, he thought, taking a deep breath before closing the gap between him and the unsuspecting woman. The time had come to prove himself worthy of the Ripper's legacy, to demonstrate that he was just as capable of inflicting terror and pain as his twisted hero.

"Excuse me," he said, his voice little more than a whisper as he approached her. "I couldn't help but notice you're all alone on this train."

The woman looked up at him, her expression unreadable in the dim light. But it didn't matter—he knew what would come next.

The fear, the panic, the realisation that she was trapped with a madman who intended to make her suffer.

Perfect, Colin thought, his excitement bubbling over like a pot left too long on the stove.

Now it begins.

Chapter Five

Colin licked his lips, his thoughts wandering to the depraved acts he could inflict upon the young woman's body before gutting her like a fish. He imagined the young woman's screams echoing through the empty train carriage, unable to escape his twisted grasp. The moment was ripe for him to indulge in his sick fantasies, and Colin couldn't contain the perverse thrill that raced through his veins as he imagined his eyes flashing with savage delight as he whipped out his concealed knife and mercilessly sliced it across her throat until her head hung backwards on her neck like a broken hinge.

The sound of her desperate gagging as the warm blood filled her lungs and she clawed blindly at her throat sent a thrill through him. With one swift movement, Colin laid her limp body on the carriage floor, raised his arm, and brought down the blade hard enough to slice through sinewy flesh until her head rolled free. Raising her lifeless head towards his face, Colin greedily stared into her eyes as her pupils rolled back in their sockets. Mesmerised by the sight of her fleshy tongue lolling from the corner of her mouth, he felt an unexpected yet undeniable urge to kiss her. He had never kissed a woman before. His nerves buzzed with frayed excitement, as he pressed his lips against hers and sunk his teeth deep into her fleshy tongue. His Adam's apple bobbed beneath his pale skin as he ripped the woman's tongue from her mouth and swallowed it whole.

He placed her head next to her lifeless body on the carriage floor. His hands shook with a trembling fury as he stripped off his coat and hung it from a nearby handrail. Kneeling beside the woman, he ripped open her dress with shaking hands, piercing her milky skin like thin tissue paper that slid away from her bones in thick glistening ribbons. Using his knife, he cut into her abdomen, releasing a hot, pungent smell that filled the air around him.

As if settling down for a feast, he knelt beside the woman's body and gorged himself on her. The young woman's innards slid between his fingers as he devoured the liver first, blood coating his chin in a grotesque display of hunger. Then her kidneys, until finally, he greedily consumed her heart, savoring its warmth upon his tongue.

His eyes glinted with savage pleasure as he devoured her ravaged body. He licked the knife before slowly and methodically slicing away her eyelids, leaving her staring in eternal horror at what he had done. Still unsatisfied, he moved around her like a vulture, licking up every drop of blood that had spilled from her body. With a satisfied smirk, he slurped his fingers clean before slipping on his coat, then turned his back on the still figure lying on the floor of the carriage. As if cloaked in mist, he vanished from sight, leaving only an eerie silence behind that lingered long into the night.

That's exactly how Colin imagined the Underground Ripper going about his deadly business. But Colin's psychopath of an idol had slain and killed many times before—he was a master at killing and butchery. Even though Colin had fantasized about this moment for months, now that it had arrived—now that he had a victim in his sights—he wasn't sure how to proceed. Perhaps he should engage her in conversation he wondered.

So, leaning against the seat opposite her, he asked casually, "Have you heard about the Underground Ripper?" His heart pounded in his chest as he studied her face, searching for any flicker of fear.

"Of course," she replied nonchalantly, barely looking up from her phone. "It's been all over the news."

"Ah," Colin sighed with disappointment at her lack of interest, but his excitement only grew. Soon, she would know firsthand what it meant to be a victim of the Ripper. "You know, they say he's never been caught because he's always one step ahead of the police. Cunning, isn't he?"

"Sure," she mumbled, her slender fingers flying across the screen as she typed out a message.

"Would you be scared if I told you I knew who he is?" Colin's voice wavered ever so slightly, but his eyes were locked on hers, hungry for the reaction he craved.

"Really? Who is it then?" She looked up at him sceptically, clearly not expecting much from this stranger's claim.

"Me," Colin whispered, his breathing heavy. "I am the Underground Ripper."

For a brief moment, there was silence. Colin held his breath, waiting for the fear to cross her face, for her to beg for her life as she realised her fate. But instead, something entirely different happened.

The young woman threw her head back and laughed—a deep, mocking laugh that made the hair on the back of Colin's neck stand on end.

She wiped a tear from her eye, and with a smirk, looked him square in the face.

"Nice try," she said, her voice dripping with sarcasm. "But if you're trying to scare me, you'll have to do better than that."

"What?" Colin's confusion was evident. This wasn't how it was supposed to go. She should be terrified, pleading for mercy as he revelled in her suffering.

"Come on," she chuckled, shaking her head. "You really expect me to believe you're the Underground Ripper?" Then eyeing the gangly and acne ridden male with the broken glasses standing before her, she sneered, "That's just pathetic."

Colin's heart sank, his excitement ebbing away as the reality of the situation settled in. His attempt at intimidation had been met with disbelief and ridicule, and now his carefully constructed plan was unravelling before his eyes. But he couldn't let it end this way. He had to prove himself—to make her see that he was every bit as twisted and dangerous as the Ripper himself.

Chapter Six

Before Colin could react, the young woman stood up and stepped closer to him. The train jolted violently as it rounded a bend in the tunnel, but she remained steady on her feet, her piercing eyes never leaving his.

"Let me show you how it's really done," she whispered, her voice suddenly cold and menacing.

"Wh-what do you mean?" Colin stammered, his heart pounding in his chest as he tried to back away, only to find himself pressed up against the closed carriage door.

"Did you really think you could fool me into believing that you're the Underground Ripper?" she asked, slowly circling him like a predator stalking its prey. "You're not a killer. You're not the underground Ripper, but I am."

Realisation dawned on Colin like a punch to the face, and his blood ran cold. He stared at the young woman in front of him, no longer seeing her as an innocent victim, but as something far more terrifying. She was the real Underground Ripper, and now he was trapped with her, alone on this late-night tube train.

"You...you're..." he stuttered, unable to form a coherent sentence.

"Surprised?" she purred, her cruel smile widening as she lunged forward, slamming Colin against the carriage door. He struggled futilely against her grip, but she held him firmly in place, her fingers digging into his flesh.

"Please," Colin begged her, his bravado gone, replaced by fear. "Don't kill me."

"Isn't that what you wanted to do to me?" she taunted him, her breath hot on his face. "You wanted to be like me, didn't you? Well, let's see how much you enjoy being killed by me."

With a swift, brutal motion, she drove a hidden blade deep into Colin's abdomen, eliciting a guttural scream from him as his body convulsed in agony. He tried to pull away, but she held him tight, twisting the knife as she carved into him with chilling precision.

"Please...stop..." Colin sobbed, his vision blurring with tears as darkness began closing in around him.

"You're pathetic," she spat, finally releasing him. "You're nothing but a wannabe."

Colin slumped to the floor, blood pouring from his mutilated body, his life slipping away as he watched the real Underground Ripper lunge at him again, driving one fist into the gaping wound in his stomach. He screamed out in agony as she grabbed a fistful of his hot, slimy intestines and yanked them from him, like she was unravelling a long length of cable. Staring into his terrified eyes, the Underground Ripper smiled as she began to strangle him with his own crimson innards.

Chapter Seven

The train driver was eager to finish his shift and head home for a much needed night's sleep. As he approached the end of the line, he braced himself for the usual routine of checking the empty carriages and making sure all the doors were locked before shutting down the train. It was tedious work, but necessary.

As he moved through each carriage, he noticed one door that refused to open. Frowning, he jiggled the handle more forcefully, only for it to suddenly give way, revealing the horrifying scene within.

A male corpse hung grotesquely from a handrail by his own intestines, his eyes wide and glassy in their final expression of terror. The word 'Wannabe' was scrawled across his forehead in blood, taunting and mocking him even in death.

"Jesus Christ!" the driver gasped, stifling

the urge to scream as he stumbled back in horror. His hands shook as he fumbled for his radio, his voice trembling as he called for assistance.

"Control, we have a major incident on board. Send police immediately. I've found a...a body."

As the words left his mouth, the driver couldn't help fighting the urge to puke at the sight of the slaughter that had taken place just a few feet from where he'd been driving the train.

The Underground Ripper had struck again, and this time, it seemed she had left a message for anyone who dared to try and copy her horrific and twisted crimes.

Sleep tight!

Dead In The Basement

For Lynda O'Rourke

Chapter One

Brian stood in the bathroom and looked at his reflection in the mirror above the sink. His breathing was deep and heavy, his breath fogging up the mirror as he stared blankly at his reflection. The house was quiet, save for the distant bark of a neighbour's dog. His tall, broad figure cast a looming shadow on the floor behind him, and his dark eyes bore the weight of secrets as he stood and stared at himself in the mirror.

Ten years of marriage to Sarah had been both a blessing and a curse. She was beautiful, with her slim figure, long blonde hair, and chocolate brown eyes. They had shared laughter and tears, arguments and make-up sessions. But the facade of their perfect life together was marred by Brian's secret affair.

"Brian..." Sarah's voice drifted from the bedroom door, soft and weary. "Are you coming to bed?"

He didn't turn around. Instead, he clenched his jaw and continued to stare at his reflection. "Yeah, just give me a minute," he replied, his voice tight with concealed emotion.

As Sarah retreated back into the bedroom, Brian's thoughts wandered to that other woman—the one who had consumed so much of his time and energy over the past six months. It was with her that he felt alive, where the excitement and intrigue of their forbidden relationship sent a thrill racing through his veins.

The affair began at the office Christmas party, when a few too many drinks led to stolen glances and whispered conversations in dark corners. Her name was Emma, a young and bubbly coworker. As the weeks had passed, their secret meetings had grown more frequent and passionate. The guilt gnawed at him every day, but he couldn't bring himself to end it. He was addicted to the adrenaline rush, the feeling of danger when he was with her.

"Is something wrong?" Sarah asked,

reappearing in the bathroom doorway. Her eyes searched his face for answers, but he offered none.

"Nothing's wrong," he lied, finally turning to face her. His expression was a mask of indifference, but internally, the storm of his deceit raged on. "I'll be there in a moment."

"Okay," she sighed, retreating once more.

The truth was that Brian's secret affair had driven a wedge between him and Sarah. His lies had piled up like bricks, building an impenetrable wall between them. He knew he couldn't keep his affair with Emma hidden forever. Eventually, the truth would come out, and everything he and Sarah had built together would crumble.

He took a deep breath, trying to steady himself before joining his wife in bed. As he walked towards the bedroom, he caught one last glimpse of himself in the bathroom mirror. For a moment, he didn't recognize the man staring back at him—the man who had betrayed the woman he once loved so deeply. What had he become?

With a heavy heart, Brian entered the bedroom, where Sarah lay waiting for him. He crawled into bed beside her, but sleep eluded him. Instead, he listened to her soft, even breathing, knowing that when the truth finally surfaced, their lives would be changed forever. And the nightmare would truly begin.

Chapter Two

The following evening after both Brian and Sarah had returned from work, the tension between them had become unbearable. Sarah had been unusually quiet since arriving home from work, and Brian could feel her questioning gaze on him as they moved around the house. He knew that she sensed something was off.

"Brian, we need to talk," Sarah said, her voice little more than a whisper as they stood side by side in the kitchen. Her hands were dusted with flour from the dough she had made for the pizza's they would have for dinner.

"Talk about what?" he asked defensively, his eyes avoiding hers as he stared at the floor.

"About us. I know you're hiding something from me," she said, her voice wavering slightly. "I can feel it. You've been distant for months now. What's going on?"

"Sarah, I told you, everything's fine,"

Brian snapped, clenching his fists at his sides. His heart raced with fear, not from his wife's suspicions but from the reality of what he'd been doing behind her back.

"Fine? You call this fine?" she shouted, tears now streaming down her face. "We barely talk anymore, and when we do, it's like talking to a stranger! I don't even know who you are anymore!"

"God damn it, Sarah!" Brian yelled, slamming his fist onto the kitchen counter, sending up a cloud of flour. "Why can't you just leave it alone?!"

"Because I love you, Brian…you're my husband…and I can't just stand by and watch our marriage be destroyed!" she says, her brown eyes brimming with tears.

In that moment, something inside Brian snapped. He couldn't bear the weight of his guilt any longer, and the thought of confessing that he'd been sleeping with another woman behind her back terrified him. Panicking and without thinking, he grabbed the knife that lay on the counter, its blade still covered with flour from the pizza bases Sarah had been cutting into slices just moments before.

"Brian, what are you doing?! Put that down!" Sarah cried out and flinched backwards in horror as she realised what was happening.

Seized by an irrational fear of having his secret affair exposed, Brian lunged towards her, his hand gripping the knife tightly. With a swift, fluid motion, he slit Sarah's throat, the sickening sound of steel slicing through flesh echoing in the small kitchen.

Blood sprayed across the room, splattering the walls and floor in bright crimson streams. In horror, Brian watched as his wife crumpled to the ground, clutching her throat. Thick hot streams of blood gushed between her fingers and red bubbles formed on her lips as she choked and sputtered out her last few breaths. Sarah lay on her back, staring up at her murderous husband, her once vibrant eyes now vacant and lifeless.

"No," he whispered, his entire body shaking as the gravity of his actions began to sink in. "What have I done?"

Chapter Three

Brian's heart pounded in his chest, the blood roaring in his ears as he stared down at Sarah's lifeless body on the kitchen floor. Panic clawed its way up his throat, threatening to choke him. He had to do something—*anything*—to hide the evidence of his gruesome crime.

"Shit, shit, shit," he muttered under his breath, fighting back the urge to puke.

His mind raced, searching for a solution, and then it hit him—the basement. With shaking hands, he grabbed Sarah's ankles and began to drag her limp form across the kitchen floor. Her once-silky blonde hair left a gruesome trail of blood behind her, the sight of which only fuelled Brian's mounting terror.

Each step seemed agonizingly slow as he struggled to haul her body down the narrow staircase leading to the basement. Sweat dripped from his brow, and he wiped it away with one bloodstained hand.

"You're heavier than you look," he grumbled through gritted teeth, then let out a shrill and depraved sounding laugh.

Once he reached the bottom of the basement stairs, Brian released Sarah's ankles with a shudder, letting her body slump onto the cold cement floor. He stood there for a moment, trying to catch his breath, but the realisation that time was of the essence spurred him back into action.

Frantically, Brian rummaged through a mound of old clothes, tossing aside a moth-eaten sweater and a faded pair of jeans until he found a tattered bedsheet. He draped it over her body, shuddering as he smoothed it down, careful to cover every inch of her pale skin. As he stood tall and looked down at her covered body, he could see blood seeping into the sheet and forming pattens like that of poppies.

"Out of sight, out of mind," he muttered irrationally, trying to convince himself that hiding her away would somehow absolve him of his sins.

Turning, he raced back upstairs and began to frantically search the kitchen for cleaning supplies. He grabbed a bottle of bleach and a scrubbing brush tucked away beneath the sink, then began to attack the bloodstained floor, desperate to erase any trace of his crime.

"God, please let this work," he muttered, his eyes flicking nervously between the clock and the stubborn red stains that refused to vanish completely.

Time seemed to crawl by as minutes turned into hours, each second bringing him closer to the possibility of discovery. Between frenzied bouts of scrubbing, he attempted to wipe his own blood-soaked hands on a dish towel, only to find that his hands were now stained crimson.

As Brian laboured over the floor, his thoughts churned like a whirlwind, each one more frantic and disjointed than the last. He knew there was no escaping the consequences of his actions, but that didn't stop him from trying. With every scrub of the brush, he prayed for a miracle—something, anything—to save him from the nightmare that his life had become.

"Please," he whispered to himself. "Please let this work."

When he was satisfied that the kitchen floor and walls no longer resembled a slaughterhouse, he stood in the center of the kitchen, his heart pounding against his ribcage like a caged animal, as his mind raced through various scenarios.

He might have cleaned away the blood, but how would he explain Sarah's sudden disappearance? He could say she had stormed off after an argument and hadn't returned or contacted him since. But would her family buy that? He knew how close she was to them and how unlikely it was that she would cut them off without a word.

"Maybe... maybe I can say she went on an

impromptu trip with friends," Brian muttered under his breath, his voice shaking with fear. "She might have been planning it as a surprise, and now she's unreachable because she's out of the country."

But even as he spoke the words, he realised the absurdity of the lie. It wouldn't take long for someone to start asking questions, digging deeper into the flimsy story he'd constructed. And then what?

Chapter Four

But there was still the matter of the body hidden in the basement. The longer it remained there, the greater the risk of discovery. Brian knew he had to dispose of it—and soon.

Descending into the basement again, the smell of musty clothes and damp earth greeted him. But there was another smell now—the acrid smell of copper—the smell of blood. He pulled out his phone, flicking on the flashlight feature. The dim glow illuminated the cluttered space, casting eerie shadows on the walls.

"Alright, let's see," he whispered, the sound of his voice nearly drowned out by the thud-thud-thud of his racing heart. "I'll need a sleeping bag or something to wrap her up in. Then I can find a remote spot to bury her."

His fingers trembled as he rummaged through old boxes, finally finding a large, weathered sleeping bag that he and Sarah had shared on the camping trips they had gone on when they had first started dating. He spread it out on the floor next to Sarah's corpse, pausing for a moment to gaze at her lifeless form.

"Sorry, Sarah," he murmured, a sudden pang of guilt washing over him. "But I can't risk having your body discovered."

He then began the gruesome task of wrapping her body in the sleeping bag, securing it with duct tape he found in a nearby toolbox. His hands shook as he worked, his stomach churning at the thought of what he was doing. Her skin already felt ice cold and the gash across her neck opened and closed like a fleshy pair of lips.

"Once I find a spot to bury her, I'll need a shovel," he said, talking to himself like he was slowly losing his mind as he tried to plan his next step. "And I'll have to make sure no one sees me. I can probably do it late at night when everyone's asleep."

As Brian finished securing the sleeping

bag, he stood back and surveyed his handiwork. The makeshift body bag lay before him, an ominous reminder of the depths to which he'd sunk.

"Shit," he whispered, his hands clenching into fists at his sides as he spotted the trail of blood on the basement floor and on the stairs where he had dragged Sarah's bloodied corpse. "I need to clean down here in the basement, too."

Just as the thought crossed his mind, he heard a loud knock at the front door. Panic flared within him, threatening to consume him whole as he stumbled up out of the basement and towards the entrance, his legs feeling like they were made of jelly.

"Police!" called a deep, authoritative voice from outside. "We've received reports of a disturbance. Can I come in?"

Brian's heart leapt into his throat as he wrenched the door open, revealing a tall, broad-shouldered Police Officer with a buzzcut and a stern expression. The man's eyes bored into

Brian's, searching for any sign of deception or guilt.

"Officer, I...I don't know who could've called you," Brian stammered, trying to sound as innocent as possible. "My wife and I had a small disagreement, but it's all settled now."

"Is she here?" the officer asked, his tone brimming with suspicion as he eyed Brian carefully.

"Uh, no." Brian hesitated. "She went out for a walk to cool off." He forced a weak smile. "I'm sure she'll be back soon."

"Mind if I have a look around?" the officer inquired, his gaze never leaving Brian's face.

"Of course not," Brian replied, stepping aside to allow the Police Officer entry, though every fiber of his being screamed at him to refuse.

As the officer stepped into the house, Brian's thoughts raced faster than ever, desperately crafting lie upon lie in an effort to save himself from the crime that was swiftly closing in on him.

Brian's pulse quickened as the officer crossed the threshold, and he tried to keep his composure. "Please, Officer, there's really no need for you to look around. My wife and I just had a small argument...it was nothing serious."

The officer paused, studying Brian's nervous demeanour. "Nonetheless, I'd like to make sure everything is in order," he said firmly, not giving Brian a chance to object further.

"Fine," Brian muttered begrudgingly, swallowing hard as he led the officer through the dimly lit house. His mind raced with thoughts of what would happen if the officer found Sarah's body or the remnants of the bloody scene, he had tried so hard to erase. He knew that if he were caught, his life would be over.

As they passed the door that led down into the basement, an eerie creak echoed through the house, causing both men to startle. Brian's heart hammered against his chest.

"Did you hear that?" the Police Officer

asked, eyeing Brian for any kind of abnormal reaction.

"It's an old house...I hear lots of creaks and bumps in the night," Brian replied dismissively.

"Are you sure your wife isn't at home?" the officer asked, stepping into the kitchen. His gaze swept about the room as he searched for any signs of trouble.

"Sarah? No, she's out taking a walk like I've already told you," Brian lied, his voice cracking slightly. He grimaced inwardly, cursing himself for sounding so unconvincing.

"Really?" the officer replied, his eyebrows raised in suspicion. "The caller mentioned hearing a woman's screams coming from this house."

"Ah, that must have been...the TV," Brian offered, attempting another weak smile. "We were watching a horror movie earlier. Must've been too loud. I apologise for that."

The Police Officer studied Brian for a

moment, his eyes narrowing as he seemed to weigh-up the plausibility of the story. "And you're sure your wife is okay?" he pressed, clearly not entirely satisfied with Brian's explanation.

"Positive," Brian insisted, forcing a confident tone. "She called me just a few minutes ago. Everything's fine."

"Alright," the officer relented, but his doubts lingered at the back of his mind. "If you're certain that everything is okay, I'll be on my way. But if you or your wife need any help, don't hesitate to call us."

"Thank you, Officer," Brian replied, eager to get him out of his house.

With his heart pounding in his chest, Brian's hands shook as he tried to steady himself. The lingering feeling of imminent doom loomed over him like a menacing storm cloud. A sudden creaking sound came from the basement again, causing him to freeze in place, his eyes darting around, searching for the source. And then he saw her, stepping from the basement and out into the hallway. It was Sarah.

Chapter Five

Brian's jaw dropped as he stared at his wife in disbelief and horror. It had been less than two hours since he'd slit her throat, and yet there she was, walking around and looking very much alive. She wore a silk scarf wrapped tightly around her neck, concealing the wound he knew must be there. He couldn't comprehend what was happening—it was impossible. The police officer followed Brian's horror struck gaze and turned around to discover Sarah standing in the kitchen doorway.

"Brian," Sarah said, her voice soft and unnervingly calm. "I thought I saw a police car parked out front as I came back from my walk. Is everything okay?"

"Y-yes," Brian stammered, unable to form any other words. He tried to avoid her gaze, but her eyes were locked on his with an intensity that made his flesh crawl.

"Are you alright?" the police officer asked Sarah, his brow furrowed with suspicion as he looked at her. "Your neighbours reported a violent row coming from this house."

"Everything is fine, Officer," Sarah replied, her voice steady as she offered a smile that seemed too sweet to be genuine. "There hasn't been any row between Brian and me. Just a little disagreement, but we're both okay."

"Are you sure?" the officer asked, scrutinizing Sarah closely. "You seem a bit...off."

"There's nothing to worry about, I can assure you," she told him, placing a hand on her silk-covered throat that hid her deadly wound.

"Alright," the officer said, although he still seemed unconvinced. He handed Sarah a card with his number on it. "Call if there are any further problems."

"Thank you, Officer," Sarah said as he left, shutting the door behind him.

Brian couldn't understand how she was alive, and the fear that gripped him was unlike anything he'd ever experienced before.

"Sarah," he whispered, his voice cracking. "How are you...?"

"Alive?" she finished for him, her voice cold and devoid of emotion. A wicked grin spread across her face as she pulled the same knife Brian had used to kill her from behind her back. "You didn't really think you could get rid of me that easily, did you?"

Brian's heart raced as she locked the front door, trapping them inside the house together. And now that the Police Officer had left, Sarah began to change—to change into the corpse that Brian knew she truly was.

In the dim glow of the moonlight filtering through the glass panels in the front door, Sarah stood before him, her long blonde hair dishevelled and matted with blood, wearing the same white blouse and jeans she had been wearing when Brian had killed her. Her eyes, once bright and full of life, were now cold and lifeless, filled with a haunting fury that sent chills down Brian's spine. Reaching up with one pale slender hand, she removed the silk scarf about her throat, revealing the bloody gash.

"Sarah?" Brian whispered, his voice trembling with a mixture of fear and disbelief as he backed slowly away from her along the hallway and into the kitchen.

"How?" Brian stammered, unable to tear his gaze from the vengeful apparition before him. The nightmarish reality of her appearance seemed too impossible to comprehend, yet there she was, as real as the fear racing through him.

Sarah moved towards him, her steps jerky and unnatural, as she crossed the creaky wooden floorboards. From the deep wound zigzagging across her throat came a wet sucking sound as she breathed in and out. Her icy stare never wavered from Brian, the man who had betrayed and murdered her in cold blood.

The kitchen seemed to shrink around Brian as Sarah closed the distance between them, the air thick with tension and suffocating dread. His heart pounded in his chest, each beat echoing in his ears like a drum signalling his impending doom.

"Brian," Sarah's voice, once sweet and melodic, now carried a hollow, haunting tone. And as she spoke the gash across her throat opened and closed like a bloody set of lips. "You took my life from me, but I can't rest until you pay for what you've done."

"What are you talking about? You're...you're dead!" Brian stammered, his voice trembling with fear.

"Dead, yes," she replied coldly, her expression void of any warmth or love they once shared, the gash across her throat making a hideous rasping sound with each word that she spoke. "But not at peace. My soul is bound to this world until justice is served. And I won't stop until you suffer the same fate you inflicted upon me."

As if guided by an unseen force, Sarah raised the knife that she held clutched in her pale hand. The blade glinted menacingly in the moonlight, like bolts of lightning blazing across the kitchen.

"Sarah, please," Brian begged, panic rising within him like a tidal wave threatening to drown him. "Don't do this. We...we can talk about this. There must be another way."

"It's too late for that, Brian," both her lips and the wound across her throat grinning, yet her eyes blazed with an otherworldly fury. "You made your choice when you betrayed me...when you killed me. Now, it's time to face the consequences."

With a swift, vengeful motion, Sarah plunged the knife into Brian's abdomen, the cold steel tearing through flesh and muscle with brutal precision. He gasped, his eyes widening in shock and pain, feeling the warm blood pour from the wound and soak his shirt.

"Sarah..." he choked out, his vision blurring as the pain threatened to overwhelm him. He placed his hands to his belly, trying to hold his intestines in his gut as they slipped and slithered through his fingers and down onto the kitchen floor, in a steaming wet pile.

In Brian's final moments, his mind raced with thoughts of regret, fear, and the knowledge that he had brought this agonizing fate upon himself.

Chapter Six

The dim glow from the television screen flickered across the living room, casting eerie shadows over the walls. On the couch, Brian's and Sarah's neighbours, Peter and Sandra, sat together, engrossed in the latest episode of their favorite crime series. The tension in the show built up to a crescendo, when suddenly, a loud bang erupted from next door, causing both of them to almost jump out of their seats.

"God damn it," Peter muttered, annoyed at the interruption. "Are Brian and Sarah at it again?"

"Seems like it," Sandra replied, her brow furrowed with worry as she stared at the shared wall between their homes. "I thought things had quieted down after that police officer left."

"Me too," Peter agreed, his concern mirroring hers. He couldn't shake the feeling that something was off next door. As another bang came from the other side of the wall, he clenched his jaw. "Should we call the police again? I mean, this is starting to sound bad."

Sandra hesitated for a moment, her mind racing. Was it their place to interfere? Were they overreacting? Her eyes darted back to the television, where the crime scene investigators were examining a victim's body. She shuddered, her heart pounding at the thought that something similar could be happening next door. But that kind of thing only ever happened on TV, didn't it?

"No, leave them to it. It's probably just another one of their stupid arguments," Sandra said, turning her attention back to the TV.

"Okay, I'm sure you're right," Peter agreed, reaching for another beer.

Little did they know that the banging noises were not a result of another argument between Brian and Sarah, but the gruesome reality of Sarah dragging Brian's lifeless body down the stairs and into the basement.

Thump!

Thump!

Thump!

Sleep tight!

Dead Doll

For Lynda O'Rourke

Chapter One

The attic was thick with dust, and the late afternoon sun streaming through the window cast eerie shadows across the room. Clara stood amidst the clutter of her father's belongings that littered the attic from floor to ceiling in old boxes. Her jeans and t-shirt, once clean, were now smeared with grime as she sorted through the remnants of her father's life. At the age of twenty-four, Clara felt that she was too young to have lost her father—her confidant and best friend. The recent death of her father to a sudden heart attack had left her grief-stricken, but she knew that the task of sorting through his belongings had to be done if she wanted to move on with her life.

"Ugh," she muttered, wiping sweat from her brow, then pulled her long blonde hair into a ponytail to keep it from falling into her eyes as she worked. With a heavy sigh, she continued placing items into cardboard boxes designated for disposal.

As she reached for an old stack of newspapers, something caught her eye. A small toy doll, worn and faded with age, lay half-buried beneath a pile of books. Clara hesitated, feeling a sudden chill creep up her spine. She knew this doll. It had been her childhood plaything, but its presence stirred memories of fear and discomfort within her.

"Hey there," she whispered, gingerly lifting the doll by its scuffed porcelain arm. "Long time, no see."

The doll stared back at her with unblinking glass eyes. Its once pristine Victorian dress was now stained and yellow like the pages of an old book, and its delicate features marred by cracks and chipped paint.

"Didn't I get rid of you years ago at a yard sale," Clara frowned down at the doll, her voice quivering slightly. "How did you end up back here amongst all this old junk?"

Clara held the doll at arm's length, examining it with a mixture of curiosity and dread. As she stared deeply into its cold, lifeless eyes, the memories of her childhood fears threatened to overwhelm her again after so many years. Images of restless nights spent staring at the doll on her shelf—convinced it moved when she wasn't looking—sent shivers down her spine.

"Maybe Dad saved you from the yard sale or something," Clara wondered out loud, trying to rationalize the doll's reappearance. But no matter how hard she tried to dismiss her unease, the memories continued to resurface—and with them, a growing sense of dread.

"Enough!" she whispered to herself, shaking her head as if to dispel the dark memories that threatened to consume her thoughts. "You're just a toy. Nothing more."

But even as she spoke the words, Clara couldn't shake the feeling that something sinister lurked beneath the dolls cracked and chipped surface—something dark and malevolent hidden within the fragile porcelain figure that gazed back at her with a sinister intensity.

Clara's heart pounded as the memories of her childhood flooded back, each recollection bringing with it an icy shudder. The doll—that dreadful thing—had had a habit of disappearing for days at a time, only to reappear in the most unexpected places, covered in dirt and grime as if it had been dragged through the mud—or perhaps the doll had dragged something through mud.

"Have you been on one your little adventures again? Is that how you managed to work your way back to this house?" Clara asked the doll, her voice a breathless whisper, as she recalled the nightmares that had plagued her as a child.

As Clara stood and held the doll at arm's length as if it might lunge at her at any moment, she could clearly recall how her childhood dreams had been filled with images of the toy stalking her, its sinister eyes watching her every move from the shadows. The worst were the nights when she'd wake up, unable to move, certain that the doll was lurking just beyond the edge of her vision, waiting for the perfect moment to strike.

"Or did Dad bring you back?" Clara's thoughts shifted to her father, and she couldn't help but feel a spark of anger at the idea that he might have kept the doll hidden all these years after she had thrown it away.

Why would he do that? But then she remembered her father telling her once that the doll had belonged to her mother—her mother who had died in a house fire just weeks after Clara had been born. Perhaps that's why her father had hung onto the doll for so long.

"Or maybe it was just one of Dad's pranks," she muttered to herself, her fingers tightening around the porcelain figure. "He knew how much I hated you."

Not wanting to hold the doll for a moment longer, Clara placed it on the floor, staring down at it as though expecting it to come to life at any moment. "So, what am I supposed to do with you now?" she asked as if the doll might just answer her.

Throw it away, burn it, bury it…anything to be rid of it, a terrified voice spoke up in Clara's mind as she stood and eyed the doll at her feet.

But the idea that her father had intentionally kept it—for whatever reason—made Clara hesitate. Was there something more to this toy than just a childhood fear?

"Ugh, you're not even worth thinking about," she muttered, trying to dismiss the growing sense of unease.

But as Clara turned her back on the doll and continued sorting through her father's belongings, she couldn't help but feel its malevolent gaze burning into her, following her every movement.

"Get a grip, Clara," she hissed under her

breath, unable to shake the feeling of dread that clung to her like a cold, clammy shroud. "It's just a stupid doll."

Yet, despite her own reassurances, Clara knew deep down that no amount of rationalization could erase the terror that had taken root in her heart. The doll, once a source of innocent play, now loomed large as an embodiment of her darkest fears. And as she labored on, the unblinking eyes of the porcelain figure seemed to watch her every move.

Chapter Two

Smoke and the scent of burning wood filled the air as Clara carried the doll to the backyard. The doll dangled from Clara's fist like a soiled thing that Clara didn't want to be contaminated by. Her heart thudded in her chest, her hand that held the doll feeling cold, yet clammy. The wind whispered through the trees, sounding like far off whispers that she couldn't quite make sense off—like voices calling out to her—warning her—from the past.

"Alright, you little monster," Clara said through clenched teeth, her voice wavering slightly as she looked down at the doll in her hand. "It's time to face the flames. It's time for me to be rid of you once and for all. My father isn't here to save you this time."

As she approached the roaring fire, the twitching and dancing flames flared heavenwards, licking at the evening sky as if urging Clara to proceed with caution. She hesitated for a moment, suddenly feeling foolish. Was she really about to burn an old toy simply because it frightened her? Was she really going to destroy a doll that night have once belonged to her mother? Perhaps she was merely projecting her own grief at her father's death onto an inanimate object.

But the unnerving memories of the doll plagued her thoughts, drowning any semblance of rationality. It was more than just a doll—it was the manifestation of her childhood nightmares—a tangible symbol of the terror that had haunted her dreams for years.

"Here goes nothing," Clara whispered, her hand trembling as she held the doll above the crackling flames.

Please, don't do this, Clara was sure she could hear the doll beg, its glassy, unblinking eyes staring up at her.

"Shut up!" Clara snapped back, the sound of her own voice startling her. "You're not real.

You don't scare me anymore!"

With a deep breath, Clara hurled the doll into the hungry flames. As the fire eagerly devoured the porcelain figure, Clara was convinced that she heard an ear-piercing scream erupt from the fire, echoing through the night like the howl of a tormented soul. Fear crept up Clara's spine, chilling her to the bone as she watched the doll's once-pristine face blacken and distort.

Pleeeease! The flames hurt! I'm dying! A voice screeched in agony from within the smoky flames.

"Did... did I just hear that?" Clara stammered, her mind racing to make sense of what she just thought she had heard. Was it her imagination, or had the doll truly screamed out in agony?

"Get a grip, Clara," she muttered to herself, though her voice was tinged with fear. "It's done. It's over. The doll is gone at last!"

But even as the words left her lips, the

terror that had consumed her since childhood refused to fade. The flames danced before her eyes, casting sinister shadows on the ground— shadows that seemed to grow larger and more menacing with each passing second. And as Clara turned to leave the fire behind, she couldn't shake the feeling that something evil still lurked within those flickering embers, waiting for its chance to return from the smouldering ashes.

Chapter Three

Clara slept at her father's house, too tired to make the long drive home. She slept in the room where she had spent so many nights as a child. And just like those nights, Clara's sleep was fitful, her dreams plagued and tormented by images of the doll as it burned in the fire. Her mind spun a twisted tapestry of nightmares where the vengeful doll stalked her through darkened hallways, its porcelain skin cracked and blackened from the fire.

"Please, leave me alone!" Clara begged in her dream, her voice a mere whisper as she stumbled along endless and never-ending corridors.

"Please," Clara sobbed, feeling the walls closing in around her. "It's over! You're gone! I killed you!"

"But did you?" The doll's voice, once sweet and innocent, now dripped with malice as it responded to Clara's pleas. "You thought you could destroy me, didn't you?"

"Stay back! Keep away from me!" Clara cried out in her sleep.

Clara's heart raced, her legs trembling and kicking against the blankets that covered her as she tried to put distance between her and the doll in her nightmares.

"Run all you want, Clara," the doll sneered, its laughter echoing through the darkness. "I'll always find you."

A shrill scream tore itself from Clara's throat as she jolted awake, drenched in sweat. She gasped for air, trying to slow her thundering heart as she scanned her bedroom for any signs of the demonic toy.

"It was just a dream," she panted and gasped to herself, feeling a shiver run through her despite the warmth of the summer night.

But her reassurances were short-lived as the eerie sound of small feet running up and down the stairs reached her ears. A chill crept up her spine as the unmistakable pitter-patter grew closer, followed by the sinister giggle of a child— a laugh that seemed to mock her every fear.

"Who's there?" Clara called out, pulling her knees to her chest, and hugging them tightly as she sat on the edge of her bed.

"Go away!" Her voice wavered, her terror growing to fever pitch as the footsteps continued their relentless approach in the direction of her bedroom.

Clara's eyes darted to her bedroom door, where a warm, almost inviting glow seeped around the edges. Her breath hitched as she noticed tendrils of smoke snaking their way into her room. She rubbed her eyes, hoping it was a trick of her mind, but the orange glow remained, accompanied by the acrid scent of burning wood.

"Please, no," Clara whispered, her voice breathless and shrill. "This can't be real."

The sound of the tiny footsteps grew louder, and the childish laughter intensified, feeding her growing fear. Clara's heart pounded

in her chest as she stared at the door, her entire
body trembling.

"Show yourself!" Clara shouted defiantly,
even though her terror threatened to swallow
her whole.

In her mind, she prayed that this was just
another nightmare. That she would wake up any
moment, drenched in sweat but safe from the
terrors her subconscious had conjured.

But as the door flew open with a violent
bang, Clara knew this was no dream.

"Hello, Clara," the smouldering doll
sniggered.

Her words were like ice-cold daggers
dripping with malice as they pierced Clara's
racing heart. There, bathed in the sinister glow of
the doorway, stood the doll. Its once innocent
face was now twisted into a grotesque smile, its
eyes gleaming with raw hate.

"Y-you..." Clara stammered, her hands
clutching at her bedsheets as if they could offer
her some protection. "You're not real. You're just

a doll."

"Am I?" the doll taunted, taking a step towards her. As it moved, Clara noticed that its once pristine dress was singed, blackened by the fire she had thrown it into. "Did you think you could escape your past so easily, Clara? Did you think you could burn away your fears?"

Clara's blood ran cold, and she felt bile rise in her throat. This couldn't be happening. It was impossible. The doll had been destroyed, consumed by flames. She had stood and watched it happen—watched as the doll had turned to nothing but a flaky pile of smouldering black ash.

"Stay away from me!" Clara shrieked, scrambling backward on her bed until she hit the wall. Her breath came in ragged gasps as she tried to make sense of what was happening.

"Your father can't protect you…not anymore," the doll hissed, stepping closer. "I made sure of that."

"What do you mean?" Clara whimpered as she cowered against the bedroom wall, the flames that were licking the edges of her bedroom doorway now crawling across the ceiling like seething fingers.

"When your father saw me again, he had a heart attack," the doll chuckled, inching closer and closer towards Clara. "The look of horror on his dying face was priceless!"

"You killed him?!" Clara hissed in disbelief.

"Just like I killed your mother," the doll giggled again. "I enjoyed watching her burn! So, it's just me and you, sweet little Clara. Now, you'll never escape me."

"Leave me alone," Clara sobbed as she learned that the doll had been responsible for taking her parents from her. Clara shuddered with sobs as she pressed herself against the wall. "Please, just leave me alone."

"Too late for that, dear Clara," the doll whispered, its voice mingling with the crackling flames that illuminated the smoke-filled air. "I'm here now. And I'm not going anywhere."

As the fire roared inside her bedroom, consuming everything in its path, Clara knew that she wasn't facing just a toy, but the embodiment of her deepest fears. The past had caught up with her, and there was no escaping it this time.

Chapter Four

The wailing sirens pierced the night, tearing through the silence as firefighters arrived at the scene of Clara's burning home. They could already see the flames licking at the windows, devouring the house from within. There was no time to waste.

"Move! Move!" the fire chief roared; his voice strained with urgency.

The fire crew sprang into action, clambering from their fire trucks, unravelling their hoses, and aiming the streams of water at the raging inferno.

Inside, Clara's mind reeled with terror. She had barely registered the doll's last sinister words when a sudden explosion of heat erupted behind her. Flames began crawling up the walls, greedily consuming her childhood memories. The room filled with choking smoke, blinding her, and stealing her breath away.

"Help me!" Clara screamed out, but her voice was swallowed by the roaring fire. She knew, deep in her heart, that no one would hear her over the cacophony of destruction.

With the doll still leering at her, Clara made a desperate decision. She lunged forward, snatching it from its perch on the edge of the bed. If this was how she was meant to die, then she would take the cursed thing down with her. She clutched it tightly to her chest, gritting her teeth against the searing pain that tore through her burnt and blistered flesh.

"Die with me," she hissed, her voice barely audible above the crackling flames that now engulfed her long blonde hair.

Clara's eyes locked with the doll's lifeless, glassy stare, and she felt a perverse satisfaction as the doll's skin began to bubble and melt under the intense heat.

Outside, the firefighters fought the blaze which was relentless. The fire chief's face paled as he realised that they were losing ground. He barked orders to his crew, trying to keep them focused on their impossible task.

"Get inside! We need to find anyone who might be trapped!" he yelled, his voice hoarse and strained.

As the fire raged around her, Clara's resolve began to waver. She wanted to scream, to cry out for help, but she knew it would be in vain. The pain was unbearable, her body ravaged by the flames. And still, she clung to the burning doll, refusing to let go.

"Clara," the doll's distorted voice whispered as its face sagged and dripped, "you can't escape me."

The firefighters finally breached the door to Clara's bedroom, stumbling upon a scene of horror. There, among the charred remnants of her life, they found Clara's burnt corpse, her arms wrapped tightly around the grotesque remains of the doll. Clara's wide and terror-filled eyes seemed to stare straight through them, as if haunted by some unseen phantom.

"Dear God," one of the firefighters muttered, crossing himself, knowing that they had arrived too late to save her, and the weight of that knowledge hung heavily on their shoulders.

And as the fire crew carried Clara's charred body from the ashes of her childhood home, the doll's blackened and warped face seemed to leer at them…a twisted smile etched into its melting features.

Sleep tight!

Dead Hands

For Val and Dave Cooper

Chapter One

John's eyelids flickered slowly open. He felt
disorientated, his mind foggy as if had been in a
deep sleep for a very long time. The sterile scent
of the hospital room filled his nostrils, and he
shifted weakly in the bed, feeling the crisp white
sheets against his skin. His head throbbed with a
dull pain, but it was nothing compared to the
searing agony that radiated from his hands.

"What happened?" John croaked, his
mouth dry, his tongue feeling like a sheet of
sandpaper.

He tried to lift his arms, wincing at the
unexpected weight and discomfort. As he finally
managed to raise them, his heart pounded in
terror. The hands before him were
unrecognizable—puffy, swollen, and sporting
blackened fingernails like they had been dipped
in ink.

"These aren't my hands," he muttered

under his breath, panic seizing him, so his chest squeezed tight. Vague memories of the accident flashed through his mind, haunting images of twisted metal and the sickening sound of crushing bones.

The railway yard had been buzzing with activity and John had been manoeuvring between two carriages, his thick work gloves gripping the greasy lever that controlled the coupling mechanism. With practiced ease, he pulled hard, expecting the satisfying clang of metal as the carriages detached. But something went horribly wrong. Instead of the usual smooth release, there was a terrifying grinding noise followed by an ear-piercing screech. In an instant, John's hands were caught in the merciless jaws of the malfunctioning machinery, the immense pressure pulverizing his fingers and palms without mercy.

Screams of horror and frantic calls for help echoed around him, but all John could focus on was the unbearable pain that consumed him.

He felt the life being drained from his body, sucked out through the mangled mess that used to be his hands. And then, mercifully, darkness enveloped him, and he knew no more.

Now, lying in the hospital bed, staring at the unfamiliar hands attached to his wrists, John couldn't help but feel an overwhelming sense of dread. He didn't know how or why these hands had come to replace his own, but he sensed something was deeply wrong with them. The pain continued to throb and pulsate through every inch of his arms, a constant reminder of his horrific-looking hands.

"Help," he whispered hoarsely, desperation lacing his voice as he stared at the grotesque appendages. "Someone, please help me."

Chapter Two

John's heart pounded in his chest as he continued to stare at the hands that were not his own. He felt as if he was being swallowed by a nightmare, unable to wake up and return to the safety of reality. The door to his hospital room creaked open, and a middle-aged doctor with graying hair and a sombre expression entered.

"Ah, Mr. Jones," the doctor said, trying to force a reassuring smile. "I'm glad to see that you're awake. How are you feeling?"

"Whose hands are these?" John demanded to know, his voice thick with fear. "These aren't mine!"

Again, the doctor tried to offer his patient a reassuring smile, running a hand through his hair. "You suffered severe injuries in the accident, Mr. Jones. Your hands... they were crushed beyond repair. We had no choice but to perform a double hand transplant."

"A... a transplant?" John stammered, his
eyes widening in shock and disbelief. "But why? I
didn't ask for this!"

"Unfortunately, we didn't have time to
consult with you," the doctor explained. "It was a
matter of life and limb. The damage to your
hands was too extensive, and there was a risk of
infection spreading through your body. A pair of
donor hands became available just in time, and
we made the decision to save your life."

As John digested the information, he
couldn't help but feel an unnatural chill creeping
down his spine. He looked down at the
unfamiliar hands again, noting their puffy,
swollen appearance. The skin was discolored
from bruising, and the fingernails were
blackened as if they belonged to a corpse.

"Will they ever look... normal?" he asked,
struggling to keep his voice steady.

"Your new hands will heal and regain
function over time, Mr. Jones," the doctor
reassured him. "The swelling and discoloration

are normal at this stage, and they will subside. The blackened nails are temporary…. a result of the surgery. They will grow out, and your hands will look more like your own."

John tried to find comfort in the doctor's words, but the gnawing fear within him refused to subside. As he stared at the grotesque appendages that now belonged to him, he wondered if he could ever truly accept them as his own.

"Rest now, Mr. Jones," the doctor said gently, placing a reassuring hand on John's shoulder. "You've been through a lot, and recovery will take time. I'll have the nurse check on you regularly, and we'll be here to help you every step of the way."

"Thank you," John whispered, unable to muster any more strength. He closed his eyes, trying to block out the horrifying image of his new hands, but sleep eluded him.

In the darkness behind his eyelids, a creeping dread festered and grew, leaving him with the unsettling feeling that something sinister was lurking just beneath the surface of his skin.

Chapter Three

Several weeks had passed since John's surgery, and though the swelling in his hands had diminished, the blackened nails and uneven stitching about his wrists remained as constant reminders that they were not his own. He found it difficult to look at them without feeling a shiver of revulsion crawl up his spine, and he wasn't the only one who noticed something amiss with his new hands.

"John, have you noticed anything...strange about your hands?" his wife, Mary, asked hesitantly one evening as they sat together on the couch.

"Strange? How do you mean?" John replied, trying to keep his voice steady despite the dread that gnawed at his insides.

"Well, for one thing," Mary began, "I saw your left hand twitch while you were sleeping last night. And yesterday, when you were reading the newspaper, your right hand seemed to be tapping out a rhythm all on its own."

"Maybe it's just my muscles readjusting after the surgery," John suggested, but the unease in his voice betrayed his real fear.

"Maybe," Mary agreed reluctantly, but her worry was evident in the furrow of her brow. "It's just that...well, sometimes it seems like your hands have a mind of their own."

John clenched and unclenched his new fists, attempting to quell the anxiety that threatened to consume him. The thought of these hideous hands acting independently of his will sent waves of terror coursing through him.

"Mary, I need to know," John suddenly said, his voice urgent. "I need to know who these hands belonged to before they were attached to me. If there's even the slightest chance that they're... I don't know, haunted or cursed or something, I need to find out. I can't live like this, always wondering."

"John," Mary replied softly, placing her

hand on his knee. "If I were you, I'd try and forget about who those hands once belonged to, or you might go insane thinking about it."

But over the following days, John couldn't stop thinking about his new hands and he became consumed with discovering the identity of the previous owner of them. And perhaps Mary had been right, he did feel like he was losing his mind, little by little each day. He scoured the internet for news articles and obituaries, searching for any clue that might lead him to the truth. His nights were filled with restless sleep, haunted by dreams of hands reaching out from the darkness to strangle him.

"John, you need to take a break," Mary implored one morning over breakfast, her voice filled with concern. "You're not sleeping, you're barely eating, and this obsession with your hands is taking over your life."

"Mary, I can't stop now," John hissed through clenched teeth, his eyes bloodshot with tiredness and his voice sounding strained. "I have to know who these hands belonged to before they were attached to me. I can't shake the feeling that there's something deeply wrong with them, and I won't rest until I find out the truth."

"Alright," she sighed, sounding defeated. "But promise me you'll talk to the doctor about this, too. Maybe he has some answers."

"Okay," John agreed reluctantly. "I'll talk to him."

But deep inside, he knew that no amount of medical reassurance would be enough to quell the growing fear that tightened its grip around his heart like a pair of cold, unyielding hands, threatening to squeeze the last breath from his body.

Chapter Four

As John sat at the kitchen table, Mary poured him a cup of coffee, her own hands steady and soothing in contrast to her husband's shaking and twitching hands.

"John," Mary began, her voice soft and cautious, "I know you're scared, but we need to face this together. Whatever is happening with your hands, I'll be here to help you through it."

"Thank you, Mary," John whispered, his throat and chest feeling tight. He glanced down at the offending limbs, bile rising in his throat. They looked so innocuous, yet he knew that beneath their swollen, bruised surface lurked something sinister.

"Here, write down what you're feeling," Mary suggested, sliding a notepad and pen across the table towards him. "Maybe it will help you process everything."

John hesitated for a moment, then picked

up the pen with his right hand. As soon as the tip touched the paper an electric shiver raced up his arm. He felt his arm tense, his fingers moving of their own accord, scrawling out unfamiliar letters in a hasty, frantic script across the notepad. *DAVID G COOPER*, his hand wrote.

"John?" Mary asked, worry creeping into her voice as she looked at the horrified expression engraved into her husband's weary face. "What's wrong?"

"Mary, I didn't write this," John stammered, his eyes wide with panic. "My hand... it moved on its own."

"Let me see," she said, gently taking the notepad from him. Her eyes widened as they scanned the name written there. "Oh, God, John. Do you know who this is?"

"No," John said shaking his head, his heart pounding in his chest. "Who is he?"

"David G Cooper," Mary explained, her voice shaking, "was better known as The Essex Strangler. He was a notorious serial killer who murdered at least seven women before he was caught and imprisoned. His signature method was strangulation, using his own hands. I would have forgotten all about it only I read an article in the paper just a few weeks ago stating that he had died in prison."

The room seemed to grow colder as the horrifying reality of John's situation settled over him like a dark, heavy shroud. The very hands that now belonged to him were once instruments of death, wielded by a merciless killer. He imagined the feel of cold flesh beneath his fingers, the desperate gasps for breath of his victims and their ultimate surrender to darkness.

"Mary," John whispered, terror clawing at his insides, "what if my hands remember? What if they want to kill again?"

"John, we'll figure this out," Mary assured him, her voice firm despite the fear that trembled within her. "We'll find a way to make this right, I promise."

But as John stared down at his murderous

hands, he couldn't help but wonder if there was any hope left for him, or if he was destined to carry on the gruesome legacy of The Essex Strangler, one life throttled out of existence at a time.

Chapter Five

That night, John's sleep was anything but restful. His dreams were plagued with vivid, horrifying images that made his heart race and his skin crawl. He found himself standing in a dimly lit alley, the damp cobblestones beneath his feet slick with rain. The air was heavy with the scent of decay, and the distant echo of footsteps seemed to be mocking him, taunting him to follow. As John moved forward, he could feel an unsettling nervous excitement building within him, as if every fiber of his being knew what was to come and yet craved it all the same.

In the shadows, a woman appeared. With her eyes wide with terror, she stumbled forward, her breaths coming in frantic gasps. As she reached out for help, John felt a sickening thrill course through him. He lunged forward, his hands shooting out to wrap around her slender neck.

"Please," the woman choked out, tears streaming down her face as she clawed at John's grip. "Please, don't..."

But John couldn't stop himself. It was as if his hands had a life of their own, tightening around her throat like a vice as the woman's struggles grew weaker and weaker. Her face turned a sickly shade of blue, and her pleading eyes bulged in their sockets. Her lips turned purple as her tongue jutted from between her lips like a bloated worm. Her bloodshot eyes stared into his, begging for mercy that would never come as Jon's hands squeezed the life out of her twitching and jerking body.

And as the last flicker of life left her puffy and swollen eyes, John felt a perverse sense of satisfaction settle over him.

"John!" Mary's voice shattered the nightmare, jolting him awake.

His heart hammered in his chest, and a cold sweat clung to his skin. But the horror of his nightmare hadn't come to an end even though he was now awake. As he blinked away the remnants of the dream, he realised that his hands were locked tight around his wife's throat.

"Mary!" John cried out, wrenching his hands away as if they'd been burned. She coughed and gasped for air, her face flushed, and her eyes filled with fear.

"John, what...what happened?" she managed to choke out, confusion and terror in her voice.

"I don't know," he whispered, staring down at his hands with a sickening dread. "I was dreaming...dreaming of killing someone, just like Cooper did. It felt so real, like I wanted it, like I enjoyed it..."

"John," Mary said, her voice trembling as she soothed her throat with one hand, "you have to fight this. You're not a killer...you're not him."

But as John looked into her frightened eyes, he couldn't help but wonder if that were still true. He had felt the darkness inside him, tasted the hunger for death that now seemed to linger in his very bones. And with every beat of his heart, he feared that his hands would once again reach out to claim another life...perhaps even the life of the woman he loved most.

Chapter Six

Determined to rid himself of the monstrous hands that had nearly murdered his wife, John leapt from the bed and sprinted down the dimly lit landing, his heart pounding in his chest with a mixture of fear and desperation. He could feel the hands twitching, as if eager to make their next kill, as he raced downstairs.

"Get away from me!" he shouted, though he knew they were a part of him now. The kitchen loomed ahead, his clenching and unclenching hands casting long and sinister shadows across the walls.

As he burst into the kitchen, his eyes locked onto the gleaming knives displayed on the magnetic strip above the counter. Grabbing the largest one, he felt its weight in his hand—a weapon capable of severing the cursed hands that threatened to betray him. The blade glinted menacingly in the moonlight filtering through the window.

"It's time to end this," he whispered, his voice shaking.

"John, don't!" Mary cried out, her footsteps echoing behind him as she ran into the kitchen. "There has to be another way!"

"Mary, I can't trust these hands anymore," he shouted in fear and desperation, his gaze fixed on the knife. "I have to do this."

"John, please!" she pleaded, tears glistening in her eyes. "Think about what you're doing! You could die!"

"I'd rather be dead than become a murderer," he said resolutely. His grip tightened around the handle of the large carving knife, adrenaline pumping through him as he prepared himself for the inevitable pain.

"Goodbye, hands," he whispered through clenched teeth, raising the knife to strike.

"NO!" Mary screamed, lunging forward to stop him. But it was too late.

With a sickening crunch, the knife

plunged deep into the flesh of his left hand. John let out a gut-wrenching scream, the pain blinding him as blood spurted from the wound, splashing his face and the kitchen walls in hot streaks. Mary's gut-wrenching sobs filled the air, but John barely heard them over the pounding in his ears.

"John, please stop!" she begged, her hands trying to pry the knife from his grip.

But he couldn't stop—not now—not with the knowledge of what those hands were capable of. John might not have wanted to stop but his hands did. As John raised the knife high in the air to bring it down on his wrist again, and sever his left hand from his bleeding wrist, the fingers of his right hand uncurled from around the handle of the blade. The knife dropped from his hand and clattered to the kitchen floor. As he stooped to snatch it up again, his fingers disobeyed him and made fists, so he couldn't take hold of it and finish the gruesome job that he had started.

Fearing that he had now lost total control of his hands, he turned to look at Mary, blood dripping from his clenched fists and all over the kitchen floor.

"Mary, I love you," he choked out, before stumbling past her and towards the door. He had to end this, once and for all.

As John staggard through the streets, blood dripping from his mutilated hand, he found himself being drawn towards the old bridge at the edge of town. The wind howled around him as his hands reached out and grabbed onto the railing, pulling him up onto the bridge. John teetered on the edge of the bridge, his bloody hands grabbing onto the handrail as he stood and stared down into the abyss below.

"Is this what you want?" he shouted at his hands, his voice barely audible above the howl of the wind that buffeted against him. "Do you want to destroy me? Well, you won't succeed!"

With that, his hand let go of the handrail, flinging John off the edge of the bridge. As he plummeted towards the raging waters below, he raised his hands to his face, the bloodied fingers twitching and jerking back and forth. In a moment of clarity, he smiled knowingly at them, realising there was no possibility of his monstrous hands continuing their murderous spree after his death.

"Good luck without me," he whispered, moments before the darkness swallowed him whole.

Chapter Seven

A hushed silence fell over the church as the mourners gathered in sombre reverence around John's coffin. The scent of incense and flowers hung heavy in the air, but it did little to lift the spirits of those gathered in the church who felt so much loss and despair at John's death.

"Dear Lord," the priest began, "we commend the soul of our brother John to your loving embrace. May he find eternal peace in your presence."

As solemn prayers were muttered, a subtle twitching disturbed the stillness of John's lifeless body within the coffin. Unnoticed by those gathered in the church, his hands began to move, their fingers wriggling like grotesque worms, seeking freedom from the stitches that bound them to his wrists.

Suddenly, a faint knocking could be heard from within the confines of the polished coffin.

Startled whispers rippled through the crowd, drawing the attention of the priest.

"Did you hear that?" one woman gasped, her eyes wide with terror.

"Is he...is he still alive?" another whispered, unable to tear her gaze away from the coffin.

The knocking persisted, growing louder and more insistent. One woman screamed, while another fainted, collapsing into the arms of her distraught husband. Believing John might still be alive, the priest hesitated for a moment before moving forward. With trembling hands, he gripped the edge of the coffin lid and slowly pushed it back.

No one could have prepared themselves for what leaped out of the casket. Two bloodstained hands emerged, their swollen, blackened fingers splayed like the legs of two monstrous spiders. Screams of horror filled the church as the hands scuttled across the floor, leaving behind a trail of crimson.

"God help us!" the priest cried, stumbling backwards, his faith shaken to its core.

"Stay away from them!" shouted a man, attempting to protect his family from the nightmarish sight.

"Is this some kind of sick joke?" another voice demanded, but the terror in his eyes betrayed his disbelief.

As the gruesome hands scuttled on their bony fingers between the pews, it was as if they possessed a sinister intelligence, knowing that their work was far from over. They seemed to revel in the chaos, thriving on the fear and panic that had engulfed the mourners in the church.

John's wife Mary, her face pale and tear-streaked, clung to her sister for support. Her mind raced with memories of John's desperate attempts to rid himself of the hands—how he had fought against them, even as they sought to use him as their instrument of death.

"John," Mary sobbed over the screams that surrounded her in all directions. "What have you unleashed upon us?"

"Mary, we need to leave," her sister urged, tugging at her arm. "We can't stay here with those...*things.*"

With one last look at John's handless corpse lying in the coffin, Mary allowed herself to be led away, unable to shake the chilling realisation that the nightmare was far from over. Mary knew what those dead hands wanted— they wanted to continue their reign of terror, strangling, and killing countless more innocent souls.

And there was nothing she, or anyone else, could do to stop them.

Sleep tight!

Toxic Snails

For Thomas O'Rourke

Chapter One

Beneath the dim, flickering light of a single, naked bulb, Thomas sat on the cold, dusty floor of his childhood home. The twenty-two year-old unemployed man had been living in the decrepit house on the outskirts of town since before he could remember. The local authority had deemed his childhood home unsafe due to the toxic waste leaking from the nearby chemical plant into the local river that snaked about the housing estate where he lived. Now, with the imminent threat of demolition looming just days away, he struggled to come to terms with the fact that he would soon be homeless.

"Where do I go from here?" he muttered to himself, running trembling fingers through his unwashed hair.

His two pet African Land snails, Gonzalo and Princess, seemed to sense the tension in the air, too. They slowly slithered their way across their makeshift terrarium—an old fish tank Thomas had found in the basement years ago.

Thomas's heart ached at the thought of leaving the only place he had ever called home. Every crack in the peeling wallpaper told a story, each creak of the floorboards whispered memories of his mother, who had passed away five years ago in her bed. Her death left him devastated, but it was her dying wish for him to care for the snails that gave him a sense of purpose.

"Mum always said you two were special," Thomas smiled as he gazed at Gonzalo and Princess. "I guess she was right."

The snails had become a bizarre source of comfort for Thomas in his darkest moments. Their slow, graceful movements and peculiar slimy beauty provided a respite from the chaos outside his crumbling sanctuary. In a world that had seemingly abandoned him, these two creatures offered him some kind of peace.

"Looks like we don't have much time left,

guys," Thomas muttered as he gazed into the tank that housed his unusual pets.

The snails had grown to an impressive size over the years, with their slimy, elongated bodies stretching to a foot long and their shells rivalling the size of footballs. He felt a sense of pride at having cared for them so diligently, feeding them salad and cucumber daily, grinding up eggshells, to sprinkle in their tank to keep their shells strong and healthy.

The creatures had been his support, their presence filling the void left when his mother had passed away. They were more than pets—they were companions, confidants, and friends. And tonight, he would have to let them go. It wasn't safe for them here anymore and he couldn't take them with him. How could he live a life of homelessness carrying around his two best friends in a large glass tank.

The late afternoon sun cast an unnatural glow over the decrepit house, casting twisted shadows on its peeling walls as Thomas paced back and forth in his bedroom, struggling to stifle a whirlwind of thoughts that threatened to consume him. The news of the impending eviction weighed heavy on his chest, like the illuminous air that surrounded the toxic river.

"Those bastards," he muttered, trembling with anger. "They're just trying to cover up their own mess."

He suspected the local authority was forcing him out of his home as a result of the chemical plant's toxic waste leakage, which had seeped into the river and endangered the health of the townspeople. Yet, all they seemed to care about was removing any trace of evidence—and that included him.

"Okay, listen up, you two," Thomas said, steeling himself for the conversation he knew he needed to have with his two pet snails. "Things are gonna change, and I don't know how to make it work. But I promise, no matter what happens, I'll find a way to keep you safe."

As he spoke, a wave of determination

washed over him. For the first time in years, Thomas felt a fire within him, one that burned with purpose and hope. He knew it wouldn't be easy, but he was willing to do whatever it took to survive and protect the creatures he had come to love.

"Mum always said we were survivors," he whispered, more to himself than to Gonzalo and Princess. "And she never lied to me. We'll find a way. We have to."

The snails seemed to understand, their antennae swaying as if nodding in agreement. Together, they faced an uncertain future, bound by their shared struggle for survival and the haunting memories of a home that would soon be nothing but dust and rubble.

Chapter Two

The sun dipped below the horizon, casting long shadows across the dusty floor of Thomas's dilapidated home. He felt the familiar weight of responsibility settle upon him as he prepared for his nightly ritual. Grabbing a handful of fresh salad and cucumber from the small refrigerator and a jar of crushed eggshells from the cupboard, he approached the large glass terrarium that housed Gonzalo and Princess.

"Alright, guys," he said softly, opening the lid and reaching in with his free hand to stroke their slimy bodies. "Dinner time."

He scattered the salad and cucumber pieces over their mossy bedding, watching as the snails' antennae twitched in appreciation of the evening meal. After a moment, they began to glide towards the food, leaving glistening trails of slime in their wake. Thomas couldn't help but marvel at their size. It was clear that the eggshells were crucial to their growth, providing essential calcium for their ever-expanding exoskeletons.

"I mustn't forget this," he smiled, sprinkling a generous amount of the crushed eggshells over their meal. The snails immediately took interest, their radulas sucking away at the calcium-rich powder.

As Thomas watched them eat, he couldn't help but worry about their future. When he was forced to leave this place, what would become of his beloved pets? They were an invasive species that could lay between one hundred and five hundred eggs every two to three months, and the potential danger they posed to the environment gnawed at him like a relentless itch.

"Maybe I can find someone who'll take you both in," he thought out loud, feeling a pang of fear tighten his chest. "But who'd want a couple of giant snails?"

Gonzalo paused in his feeding, his antennae swaying as if in response to Thomas's concern. Princess, however, seemed oblivious, her body pulsating rhythmically as she devoured the eggshells.

"Damn it," Thomas muttered through gritted teeth, his eyes welling up with tears. "I can't just leave you two here. But I can't set you free either. You could destroy everything."

He leaned against the terrarium, his head spinning with the weight of his dilemma. The snails continued to eat, their slow, methodical movements a stark contrast to the turmoil that raged within him. As he gazed at them, he knew that he had to make a decision—a decision that would determine not only his own fate but also that of the creatures who had become his only companions in a cold and unforgiving world.

Thomas clenched his fists, determined to protect his pets. They deserved better than this bleak and pointless existence. "Tonight," he said with resolve, "I'm setting you both free."

Chapter Three

Moonlight slanted through the branches overhead as Thomas stood in the middle of the wood, the large glass tank that housed his snails cradled in his trembling arms. The night before his eviction had come too quickly, leaving him with little choice but to carry out the heart-wrenching decision he felt he had been forced to make.

"Okay, guys," he whispered, over the sound off leafy branches swaying overhead. "This is it."

He knelt down and opened the glass tank, revealing Gonzalo and Princess, their shells glistening beneath the silvery light. As they slid out onto the wet grass, Thomas couldn't help but notice how the darkness seemed to swallow them up, as if the world itself was eager to erase any trace of their existence.

"Be safe," he urged them, his eyes welling

up with tears. "I'm so sorry."

Slowly, he turned away, his heart aching with regret. But as he took his first step back towards his soon-to-be-demolished home, a distant memory flickered in his mind—one of news reports and whispers of toxic waste from the nearby chemical plant seeping into the river.

Thomas woke with a start, his sheets damp with sweat. The images from his nightmare lingered in his mind—Gonzalo and Princess writhing in agony, their once-glistening shells now corroded and crumbling, the toxic waste pulsing through their bodies like venom. Horror clawed at his chest as he realised the gravity of his mistake.

"God, what have I done?" he cried out, untangling himself from his filthy and stained bedding, and sprung from his bed.

The moon was dipping in the sky and Thomas knew there was not a moment to lose. He threw on his shabby clothes, grabbed a torch, and raced out the door, his heart pounding with urgency.

"Please, let them be okay," he whispered to himself as he retraced his steps back into the woods where he'd left his beloved pets. "I'll never forgive myself if something happens to them."

The woods seem to come alive around him, shadows dancing beneath the canopy of leaves, the wind carrying whispers of unseen creatures. Fear gripped him, but he pushed forward, determined to find Gonzalo and Princess before it was too late.

"Princess? Gonzalo?" he called out, his voice trembling. "I'm so sorry. I shouldn't have left you here."

As he made his way deeper into the woods, Thomas noticed an eerie glow near the riverbank. His heart leaped into his throat as he recognised the sickening yellow light—the telltale sign of the toxic waste that had poisoned his town.

"No, this can't be happening," he choked

out, fear rooting him to the spot. "I didn't realise I had set Princess and Gonzalo free so close to the river. What have I done?!"

But then, a glimmer of hope. A faint trail of slime glistened in the rays of silvery moonlight.

"Come on," he urged himself, following the trail. "I can still make this right."

As he followed the thick slimy trail, he called out to his precious snails, praying for some sign of their survival. But as he drew closer to the river, a sinking feeling filled is stomach like a slab of concrete.

"Please, guys, don't be near the water," he whispered, panic rising up his throat.

The trail led him to a small clearing by the riverbank, and there, illuminated by a single shaft of moonlight, were Gonzalo and Princess.

He froze in horror at the sight before him. The once familiar forms of his cherished snails were now grotesque monsters. Their shells, once nearly the size of footballs, now towered over their enormous, wet, bloated bodies. Their glistening flesh pulsated with an unnatural, sickly yellow glow, and their eye stalks had grown as thick as human arms, slithering through the air like serpents.

"Oh my God... what happened to you?" Thomas's voice trembled, as he stared at the monstrous creatures that were once his beloved pets.

Chapter Four

The mutated snails seemed to sense his presence and turned towards him, their newly elongated eyestalks swaying menacingly. Fear gripped Thomas as he took a step back, his heart hammering in his chest.

"Please... please don't hurt me," he whispered, his voice cracking with terror. He looked into the eyes of the creatures that were once his family and prayed they would remember him.

The snails, however, no longer recognised their former caretaker. They only saw a potential threat—or possibly prey. As they began to inch closer to Thomas, their monstrous forms filling his vision, he realised the horrifying truth—the toxic waste had not only destroyed his home but had also turned his pets into nightmarish creatures.

"Forgive me," Thomas blurted out, tears

streaming down his face, as he backed away from the advancing snails, his legs trembling beneath him. "I never meant for this to happen."

With unnatural speed, the snails lunged towards Thomas, their grotesque bodies propelled by muscular contractions that left him no time to react. He stumbled backwards, his feet slipping in the mud, and fell with a squelchy thud onto the ground. The mutant creatures closed in on him with alarming speed.

"NO!" Thomas screamed as one of the snails reached him, its bloated body pressing down onto his chest, squeezing the breath from his lungs. Its colossal shell cast a dark shadow over him, blocking out the moonlight. He could hear the sickening squelch of its flesh as it slithered across his body, pinning him in place beneath its colossal weight.

"Please... don't," Thomas gasped, his eyes wide with terror.

But his plea was met with indifference. The snails were driven by an insatiable hunger that had been awakened by the toxic waste, and they would not be satisfied until they had devoured every ounce of Thomas's bones.

The second snail joined the first, its massive body acting as a suction pump, holding Thomas down even as he thrashed about in agony. He could feel the creatures' rasping radulas scraping against his skin, peeling away the layers of flesh to expose his bones. His desperate screams echoed through the night, swallowed up by the darkness.

"Help me!" Thomas screamed out, his voice raw with pain and fear.

But there was no one to help him—all the nearby houses had long been vacated. Unlike Thomas, all the local residents had heeded the warnings of the local authority and left their homes. Only Thomas had refused to leave and now his life had become a living nightmare—a nightmare that there was no waking from.

Thomas's mind raced, seeking an escape from the unbearable horror. He tried to focus on the memories of his childhood home and his mother, the laughter shared with his pets when they were still small and harmless. But those memories were now lost forever by the monsters that were devouring him—sucking and slurping his flesh from his bones.

As the snails continued their gruesome feast, Thomas's consciousness began to fade. His agonised screams echoed through the night as the mutated snails continued to feast on his bones, their grotesque forms writhing and glistening in the moonlight. The toxic slime that oozed from their pulsating bodies now served as a gruesome cocoon, enveloping his body, and dissolving his flesh.

"Please... make it stop," Thomas whimpered, his voice raw and broken.

But there was no mercy to be found in the eyes of Gonzalo and Princess, their snake-like eyestalks blazing with an insatiable hunger.

"Help me..." Thomas begged, but the words were drowned out by the sickening sound of the mutant snails sucking flesh from his bones.

His mind raced, desperate for any semblance of hope or relief from the unending torment. But all he could find was darkness—suffocating, impenetrable darkness.

Chapter Five

With their grisly meal complete, the snails released Thomas's limp, boneless form. What remained of him resembled nothing more than a deflated sack of flesh, a horrifying testament to the creatures' newfound appetite. The snails, now even more grotesque and swollen from their meal, sensed the stirrings of hunger within their bloated bellies once again. They turned their attention to the house that lay in the distance, the place where they had been nurtured, and where more sustenance awaited them.

With frightening speed, the snails surged towards Thomas's home, their tank-like shells smashing and breaking apart the doorway as if it were made of brittle glass. Their massive, pulsating bodies forced their way up the narrow staircase, leaving a glowing trail of toxic slime behind them. The familiar walls and rooms of

Thomas's house crumbled under the weight of the monstrous creatures.

The snails could sense something else within the house, something that would nourish their hundreds of recently laid eggs growing in the toxic waste. They were no longer satisfied with just devouring bones—they needed more. And they would not stop until they had consumed every trace of human life that crossed their path, leaving only death and despair in their wake.

The snails' eye stalks, as thick and sinewy as grown men's arms, undulated in the dim glow of the bedroom. The sight of the decaying corpse on the bed sent ripples of revulsion down their slimy bodies. Thomas's mother lay there, her once warm and loving features now barely recognizable beneath the putrid mass of maggot infested and rotting flesh. Though they had feasted on Thomas with voracious hunger, even these monstrous creatures seemed repelled by the stench of death that filled the air.

Such a waste, Gonzalo almost seemed to hiss, his voice a sickening slurping and sucking sound. *If her body wasn't so rotten, she could have been food for us.*

Us, and our children, Princess replied, her voice sounding like a gargling rattle. *We owe it to our unborn hatchlings to find better sustenance.*

As they communicated in their own distorted voices, Thomas's house creaked and groaned under the immense weight of the mutant snails. Their massive shells scraped against the ceiling, sending flakes of plaster cascading down onto the floor.

Let us leave this place, Gonzalo hissed, turning his grotesque gaze toward the shattered doorway. *There is nothing more for us here.*

Agreed, Princess gargled. *The night awaits, and with it, more bones to sate our hunger.*

A shared sense of urgency gripped them, fuelling their determination to find fresh bones. They could feel the hundreds of eggs they had laid by the river, growing rapidly in the toxic waste, and demanding sustenance.

Must... find more, Gonzalo slurped, his body pulsating with hunger.

We can't let our children starve, Princess added, her voice sounding like she was gargling on a throat full of water.

With a throbbing shudder of rippling wet flesh, the snails withdrew from the room, leaving the decaying corpse of Thomas's mother untouched. As they squeezed their way back down the stairs, the house protested further, sagging under the strain.

Imagine the feast we'll have when our numbers grow, Gonzalo whispered, his thoughts focused on the hundreds of eggs gestating in the toxic waste. *No human will be safe.*

Indeed, Princess agreed, as they slithered out into the darkness. *They will all come to know the terror we bring.*

The toxic snails vanished into the night, their luminescent glow fading into the inky blackness. The house, now little more than a crumbling ruin, stood as a silent testament to the horrors that had taken place within its walls. And while the snails had left this place behind, their hunger for human bones would not be easily sated. They would continue to grow and multiply, an ever-present threat lurking just beyond the edge of sight.

As they ventured forth, driven by an insatiable need to feed their growing brood, the wind carried away their sinister whispers, leaving only the chilling silence of a world forever altered by their monstrous transformation.

Sleep tight!

Chapel Girl

For Zachary O'Rourke

Chapter One

Zach's heart pounded as he crept along in the shadows behind Jessica, the enigmatic girl he had become infatuated with since he had first laid eyes on her. The dimly lit corridor he now crept along seemed to stretch on endlessly, its walls decorated with stained-glass windows and eerie portraits that appeared to watch every cautious step that he took in pursuit of Jessica. But however much the watching portraits made his flesh crawl, he refused to turn back. He was driven by a mixture of love and curiosity. Zach couldn't resist the urge to follow Jessica, even though he knew that stalking her like this was wrong—if not a little creepy.

Jessica looked as if she had stepped from the pages of a gothic novel, her beauty both alluring and strangely unsettling. Her long, raven-black hair cascaded down her back in thick glossy waves, framing a face so smooth and pale it looked as if it had been carved from porcelain—like a doll which held an air of melancholic beauty. She wore a lacy black blouse, with sleeves that billowed at the wrists like tendrils of smoke, paired with a high-waisted skirt that hugged her slender hips before flaring out just above her knees. Her legs were covered with black stockings, which led down to a pair of scuffed leather ankle boots—the perfect finishing touch to her dark and gothic appearance. As she walked, the sound of her heels clacking against the stone floor echoed through the corridor, sending shivers down Zach's spine.

Despite this, every step she took fuelled his desire to uncover the truth about this mysterious girl who had captivated him so completely. Even as the whispers which had circulated among their classmates that painted her in a negative light—hinting at secrets best left undiscovered—Zach couldn't tear his eyes away from her. He knew that people talked about her family's poverty and how she bought her clothes from the flea market—and worst still, how Jessica was in some way responsible for the unexplained disappearances of several of their classmates.

But none of that mattered to Zach. In his eyes, she was a living incarnation of the forbidden and the mysterious. She had a dangerous beauty that called to him like a moth to a flame. And so, he crept along in her shadow, taking care not to make a sound as he followed her deeper into the darkness.

A sudden streak of purple lightning forked across the night sky outside, illuminating the corridor for a brief, but intense moment. Zach's heart thundered in his chest as he caught a glimpse of Jessica's dark silhouette against the stone walls. The eerie flash of light was followed by the echoey snap of her heels, which seemed to grow louder and more urgent with each step she took.

"Damn," he whispered under his breath,

his pulse racing in sync with the click-clack of her footsteps.

Jessica stopped abruptly, her thin gasp of surprise barely audible over the rumble of distant thunder. She turned her head slightly, as if trying to catch a glimpse of an unseen presence lurking in the shadows. Zach pressed himself against the wall, holding his breath, hoping that she wouldn't notice him.

Believing that she was alone, Jessica hastened her pace towards her destination—the chapel. Her movements were swift and graceful, like a predator stalking its prey. The enigmatic girl didn't seem fazed by the storm raging outside or the watchful gaze of the haunting portraits—if anything, it appeared to spur her on.

Where is she going? Zach wondered to himself, his curiosity getting the better of him as he continued to follow her. He knew that there was something different about Jessica, something inexplicable that set her apart from everyone else. And he was determined to find out what it was, no matter the cost.

As he watched Jessica reach the entrance to the chapel, another bolt of purple lightning struck, casting an unnatural glow through the stained-glass windows. The sudden brightness revealed the ornate wood carvings on the doors, depicting scenes of angels and demons locked in an eternal battle. Jessica pulled open the chapel door and with one fleeting glance back over her shoulder, she disappeared inside like a fleeting wisp of smoke.

"So, is this where I'll finally learn your secret, Jessica?" Zach whispered to himself, his heart pounding.

With a deep breath, he snuck from the shadows and pushed open the door, following the sound of her footsteps echoing through the hallowed chapel.

Chapter Two

Zach's heart raced, his thoughts a swirling vortex of emotions as he trailed behind Jessica. He couldn't help but be captivated by her and it wasn't just her otherworldly beauty that had ensnared him—it was the enigma that shrouded her very existence.

Jessica, wait! he called out in his mind but dared not utter out loud. His love for her, though one-sided and unspoken, fuelled his desire to uncover the secret that she seemed so desperate to keep hidden from prying eyes.

The other students had spoken ill of Jessica, whispering cruel taunts and rumours about her being in some way responsible for the disappearance of Melody Jones, Harry Clarke, Beatrice Law, and several other students. But they had just left the school—moved on to someplace else. So, unlike the rest of his classmates, Zach saw something in Jessica that they didn't—or perhaps couldn't. He saw the strength in her eyes, the defiance in her posture, and the determination in her stride.

Am I the only one who sees this? he wondered, feeling a pang of sadness but deep down a secret satisfaction at the thought that he might be alone in his admiration for her. Zach quite liked the idea that he was the only one— the only boy at least—who could see her beauty.

Where are you going, Jess? he silently questioned, ducking behind a stone pillar to avoid being spotted as he followed her deeper into the chapel. The air grew colder with each step, the faint scent of damp earth and mildew stinging his nostrils.

Are you really so terrible? he pondered, remembering the harsh words of his classmates. *Or are they just blind to your true beauty?*

Please, let me in, Jess, he mentally begged, feeling an almost overwhelming need to protect her from the harsh words, suspicions, and cruel taunts that she had to endure. *Let me share your burden...let me share your secret, whatever that might be.*

He knew that the answers he sought lay within the dimly lit chapel, and with each step, he inched closer to understanding the mysterious girl that haunted his every waking thought. However, there was no turning back now, no matter how dark or twisted the truth might be

"Jessica," he whispered under his breath, his voice barely audible above the sound of his heart pounding in his chest. "Whatever your secret might be...I won't give up on you."

As Zach continued to follow Jessica through the overwhelming gloom of the chapel, he could not shake the feeling that something sinister awaited them both in the shadows.

And as the storm outside raged on, the echoes of their footsteps and the whisperings of his own thoughts mingled into a haunting symphony of the unknown.

Chapter Three

Zach's heart raced as he admired Jessica's beauty from a distance, an ethereal glow seeming to surround her in the dimly lit chapel. He felt an almost magnetic pull towards her, his body involuntarily moving closer with each step he took.

"Jessica," he whispered softly again, reaching out from the shadows to brush against her arm ever so slightly as he inched closer to her, hoping to capture her attention without startling her.

Suddenly Jessica turned her head, eyes wide with surprise, but didn't say anything. Instead, she gave Zach a fleeting look before quickening her pace.

"Wait!" Zach called out, panic rising in his chest at the thought of losing her in the labyrinth of shadows that smothered the chapel from wall to wall.

But she didn't stop, and so he hastened his step to keep up, his mind racing with questions about what could possibly be driving her into the dark recesses of the chapel.

The disquieting atmosphere intensified as they entered the main chamber. Dim lighting was provided by a cluster of candles that flickered wildly, casting freaky shadows upon the grey stone walls. The worn cobble stones beneath their feet seemed to be stained by the anguish of the countless souls who had come to seek solace within these hallowed walls, and the stained-glass windows depicted scenes of torment and redemption that sent gooseflesh down Zach's spine.

"Jessica," he tried again, forcing his voice to remain steady despite the fear gnawing at the edges of his sanity. "Please, don't run from me. I'm not like the others…I want to be your friend. I just want to help you."

She paused for a moment, visibly conflicted, before turning to face him. In the wavering candlelight, her eyes glistened with unshed tears, and Zach's heart clenched painfully as he realised the depth of her pain caused by the harsh taunts and rumours spread by their classmates.

"Zach," she whispered, her voice trembling with a vulnerability he had never heard before. "I don't know if you can help me. I don't know if anyone can."

"Let me try," he pleaded, reaching for her hand, and holding it tightly within his own. He fought the urge to flinch away at the iciness of her touch. "Whatever your secret is, whatever burden you carry, I want to share it with you."

As the storm outside continued to roar and fill the night sky with tongues of forked lightning, the echoes of the thunder and driving rain against the spire of the chapel roof, mingled into a haunting song of the dead. And in that moment, Zach vowed to stand by Jessica's side, no matter what horrors the truth of her secrets might reveal.

They stood in silence and looked at each other, as rain pelted the ancient stone walls and stained-glass windows of the chapel. Zach's breath fogged before him, his skin overrun with gooseflesh as the chill of the chapel clawed at him like icy fingers. Then without a word, her hand slipped from his and she disappeared once more into the shadows that shrouded each corner of the chapel like vast inky cobwebs.

His heart hammered in his chest, as he tiptoed forward in pursuit of her once more.

"Jessica," he whispered, her name barely audible above the roar of the storm. He knew she was there, somewhere in the darkness—he could feel her, an almost magnetic pull towards the girl who held his heart captive.

As Zach crept between the pews, he did his best to keep his movements silent and his breathing steady. He knew Jessica was hiding something, and though he longed to protect her from whatever burden she carried, he couldn't ignore his own morbid curiosity. Love and fear intertwined, fuelling his determination to uncover her secret.

"Help me, please," came the faint echo of her voice, bouncing off the stone walls and leaving him momentarily disoriented. It sounded as if her voice was coming from everywhere and nowhere all at once.

"Where are you?" he called back, trying to inject confidence into his trembling words.

"Here," she replied, the word barely more than a breath, but enough for Zach to pinpoint her location.

He approached cautiously, waiting for any sounds that might indicate danger or warning. His hands shook with a mix of anticipation and dread, the weight of uncertainty pressing down on his chest like a dead weight.

"Jessica," he whispered again, finally reaching her side. In the dim light, her eyes were wide and fearful, and for the first time, Zach saw the vulnerability behind her mysterious facade.

"Zach," she whispered. "You shouldn't be

here."

"Whatever it is you're hiding, whatever is causing you pain," he told her, "I want to help."

"Can you really?" she asked, something dark and desperate flickering in her gaze. "Even if it terrifies you?"

"Especially if it terrifies me," he replied, his determination stronger than the fear gnawing at his bones.

And as he stood in the cold and shadowy embrace of the chapel, Zach knew that there was no turning back.

Chapter Four

The dim candlelight flickered across Jessica's face, casting eerie shadows that seemed to dance with her every breath. She hesitated for a moment, her eyes locked on Zach's, as if silently pleading for understanding. Then she slowly reached into the pocket of her second-hand skirt and pulled out a small, wrapped package.

"Promise me," she whispered, her fingers trembling as they gripped the paper. "Promise me you won't judge me or turn away."

"I promise," Zach nodded, his heart pounding in his chest.

He had come this far, driven by his love and curiosity for this strange, yet captivating girl and he wouldn't back down now.

Jessica unwrapped the package with shaking hands, revealing a sandwich cut neatly into two halves. The bread was slightly stale, its edges curling up from age, but it was what lay between the slices that made Zach's breath hitch in his throat.

A freakishly fat, black spider wriggled frantically amidst a smear of mayonnaise, its hairy legs kicking uselessly against the confines of its edible prison. Zach felt bile rise in his throat as he watched the grotesque creature struggle for freedom, his mind unable to comprehend why Jessica would carry such a thing with her.

"See?" Jessica murmured, tears streaming down her face as she lifted one half of the sandwich towards her lips. "This is my secret, Zach. This is my curse."

"Jessica," Zach stammered, horrified yet unable to look away. "What are you doing? Why are you going to eat that spider?"

"Because I must," she choked out, before taking a large bite of the sandwich, the spider's legs still twitching as she chewed. Her face twisted in disgust, but she swallowed determinedly, tears streaming down her cheeks.

"It's the only way to keep them at bay."

"Them?" Zach asked, his voice barely audible in the cold, oppressive silence of the chapel.

"Spiders" she whispered, her voice quivering with terror. "They feast on fear, and I...I have to feed on them...I have to eat this monstrosity, so they don't consume me."

Zach stared at her, his mind racing with questions and horrified fascination. The love he felt for Jessica wavered with the revulsion that threatened to overwhelm him. Finally, he made his decision.

"Let me help you," he said, his voice hoarse but determined. "Let me share your burden."

"Zach, no!" Jessica protested, her eyes widening in horror as he reached for the remaining half of the sandwich.

"Jessica, I promised," Zach reminded her, his hand shaking as he lifted the sandwich to his lips. "I won't judge you or turn away. This is what true love means."

And with that, he took a bite, feeling the spider's legs brush against his tongue and gagging as its body crunched between his teeth. He fought the urge to vomit, forcing himself to swallow the vile concoction while Jessica watched him, tears streaming down her face.

"Thank you," she whispered, her voice choked with emotion as she offered him the remainder of the sandwich. "Thank you for not leaving me alone…alone with the spiders."

As Zach accepted her offering, the shadows of the chapel seemed to grow darker and more menacing. He stuffed the remainder of the sandwich between his lips, the twitching and jerking legs of the half-eaten spider scratching the back of his throat as he swallowed it down. He tried to hide his grimace and forced a smile instead at Jessica.

"That didn't taste so bad," he said, trying to sound bold and brave when all he wanted to do was scream.

"I bet you'll be even tastier than the others," Jessica suddenly sneered at him. Her once sweet and alluring smile now gone from her soft pouting lips.

"I... what?" Zach whimpered, his blood turning to ice in his veins.

"It's nothing personal," Jessica said menacingly, her back now bristling with eight thick, long and black hairy legs.

"What the hell is happening here?" Zach stammered, backing away from her as fast as he could.

Using her eight spider-like legs, Jessica skittered quickly towards him. "It's nothing personal, Zach, it's just what spiders like me do when they get their prey ensnared in our webs."

"Which is what exactly?" Zach gasped, frantically looking for an escape route.

"Eat them, my precious one. It's a real honour actually. Female spiders of my kind only consume the finest victims and you are by far the most prime that I've ever had in my web."

Jessica grinned wickedly, her lips splitting into a wide grin to reveal a set of needle-sharp fangs dripping with venomous saliva. "I've consumed many before you..." she crowed triumphantly and glanced upwards.

Zach gulped hard trying to maintain his composure, stumbling backwards until he collided with a pew. He felt the icy fear in the pit of his stomach as he followed Jessica's gaze. His eyes fell upon the shadows high above, shifting and swaying like curtains pulled by an unseen ghostly hand. The realisation hit him like a punch—it was cobwebs, hosting hundreds, perhaps thousands of spiders. As they fluttered aside, he stumbled backwards in horror. Hidden behind them were crimson stained mummies of his classmates. They hung from tangled webs, half-eaten bodies, open mouths, and sunken eye sockets writhing with spiders. Through the rot and ruin Zach recognised Melody Jones, Harry Clarke, Beatrice Law, and other students that had once filled the halls of his school.

Realisation dawned on Zach like a sledgehammer. The rumours about Jessica were true, and he had made a terrible mistake by coming here. He spun around frantically, trying to flee from the chapel and the mutant spider that now stood behind him on eight hairy legs. But before he could even take a step towards the chapel doors, he was pulled back with great force. As Zach tried to scream, his throat ran dry with fear.

He looked down to see his legs ensnared in sticky webs, and another thread wound tightly around his waist as he was yanked up into the air. Struggling against the silky restraints, Zach watched helplessly as the spider-girl approached him at lightning speed, her black legs tapping menacingly against the stone floor. In mere moments she had spun him up tight in her unbreakable web, her poisonous fangs glistening hungrily.

"It's nothing personal," she hissed, spraying him with venom.

The monster would have her way with him, and there was no escaping it.

Sleep tight!

The Man Who Ate Himself To Death

For Joseph O'Rourke

Chapter One

Joseph sat alone in his dimly lit living room, the fringe of his unkempt brown hair almost hiding his dark rimmed eyes. The flickering light from the television cast peculiar shadows across the dingy walls as he absently chewed at his fingernails. On the screen, an old black-and-white horror film played—a vampire lunged at its victim, fangs bared to sink into pale female flesh.

"Blood never tasted so good," the vampire's sinister voice echoed out of the TV set, sending gooseflesh scampering down Joseph's spine.

His nervous habit of biting his nails had started years ago as a child, but now at the age of twenty-seven it had escalated to something far more compulsive and insidious. It was as though the taste of his own blood had become a craving, a hunger that gnawed at him incessantly. He couldn't remember when he had last eaten anything else, the thought of food was repulsive compared to the metallic tang of his own blood.

There were times when he bit them unconsciously, like that night two weeks ago at the movie theatre. He had been watching another horror film, one where the protagonist fought off hordes of zombies with nothing but a chainsaw and sheer determination. As the tension built, Joseph had found himself chewing not only his nails but the surrounding skin, leaving bloody crescents in the tender flesh. He hadn't even noticed until the warm, coppery taste filled his mouth, pulling him out of the on-screen gore and back into reality.

Now, as the vampire on TV savoured the victim's blood, Joseph's teeth grazed over one of his already ragged fingernails. A small droplet of red welled up from the torn edge, and he brought it to his lips, unable to resist the temptation.

"Damn it," Joseph muttered, wincing at the sharp pain radiating from his fingertips.

His attention was drawn away from the TV as he felt a slow drip of blood rolling down his hand. With horror, he realised he had chewed off the very tip of his forefinger, leaving nothing but a raw, throbbing stump. The pain was intense, yet somehow it only served to heighten the perverse pleasure he derived from this self-mutilation.

"God, why can't I stop?" Joseph thought, staring at the mangled remains of his finger with a mixture of revulsion and fascination.

He brought the bloody digit to his lips, unable to resist the allure of his own flesh. As he tasted the coppery tang of his blood mixed with the raw meat, he felt a sick thrill coursing through him. The texture was unlike anything he had ever experienced, and the taste—rich, salty, and undeniably his own—sent shivers down his spine.

"Maybe just one more bite," he whispered to himself, his voice trembling with both fear and excitement.

Gripping his thumb between his teeth, he bit down hard, determined to satisfy the gnawing hunger inside him. His teeth shredded through skin and muscle, the pain intensifying with each new tear. But instead of faltering, Joseph found himself fuelled by the agony—it only served to deepen his craving.

"God, it tastes so good," he thought, momentarily forgetting the horror of what he was doing. As he continued to consume his own flesh, the grisly scene on the television paled in comparison to the monstrous act taking place in his living room.

In this self-destructive spiral, Joseph felt both prisoner and master, unable to resist the perverse allure of his own body. And as the vampire screeched triumphantly on screen, he couldn't help but wonder if, in some twisted way, he had become a monster just as terrifying.

Chapter Two

The first light of dawn crept through the curtains, casting a muted glow over the living room. As Joseph stirred, the throb in his right hand pulled him from the depths of sleep. His eyelids fluttered open, and for a moment, he felt disoriented, unsure of how he had ended up on the sofa.

"Jesus," he groaned, trying to shake off the fog of unconsciousness. Blinking against the dim light, he lifted his right arm, only to be met with a sight that made bile rise in his throat.

Where his right hand should have been, there was nothing but a gnarled, bloody stump. The mangled remains of his wrist were coated in dried blood, the jagged edges of bone protruding grotesquely from the torn flesh. Panic set in as the reality of the situation sank its teeth into his mind.

"What the hell?" he choked out, staring at

the horrific sight before him. "I didn't... I couldn't have..."

His heart pounded like a jackhammer in his chest, threatening to burst from the sheer force of his terror. Desperate to staunch the flow of blood and ease the searing pain, Joseph stumbled to his feet and made a frantic dash to the bathroom.

Each step left a crimson footprint on the tiled floor—a grisly trail marking his path. He could feel the wetness between his toes as he moved, the sticky sensation only adding to his mounting panic.

"Think, think, think!" he muttered to himself, his breaths coming in short, ragged gasps. "What do I do? What the hell do I do?"

He reached the bathroom, flicking on the light switch and wincing as the harsh fluorescent glare assaulted his eyes. The reflection in the mirror showed a man teetering on the edge of sanity, his face pale and drawn, sweat beading on his brow.

"Okay, okay," he whispered, trying to muster some semblance of courage. "I've got to clean this up."

He turned on the tap, letting the cool water cascade over the mutilated remains at the end of his wrist. The sensation was both numbing and agonising, as if ice and fire were waging a war beneath his skin. He gritted his teeth, determined not to let the pain get the better of him.

"I can't... can't just leave it like this," he thought, his mind racing with a cruel mix of dread and urgency. "Need to wrap it up...stop the bleeding."

Spurred into action, Joseph grabbed a clean towel from the rack and pressed it against the stump, wincing as the fabric absorbed the blood and clung to his mangled flesh. He knew it was only a temporary solution, but for now, it would have to do.

"God help me," he grimaced through clenched teeth. "What have I done to myself?"

As he stared at his bandaged wrist, he couldn't shake the memory of the previous night—the taste of his own flesh, the perverse thrill that had possessed him. And in the pit of his stomach, a gnawing hunger still lingered, eager to consume whatever horror awaited him next.

"Doctor...I need a doctor," Joseph mumbled to himself, the realisation hitting him like a ton of bricks.

He fumbled for his phone with his remaining hand and dialled the number of his local clinic. His heart raced as he waited for someone to pick up.

"Doctor Brown's office," a calm and soothing voice finally answered.

The voice belonged to a middle-aged woman who had been working at the clinic for years. Her steady tone brought a small sense of relief to Joseph's panicked state.

"Hi, uh, I need to see Doctor Brown as soon as possible," Joseph stammered out, unable to hide the urgency in his voice. "It's an emergency."

"Of course, let me see when we can fit you in," the receptionist replied professionally, unfazed by Joseph's distress. "We have an opening in thirty minutes. Will that work for you?"

"Yes, thank you," Joseph said, his voice trembling.

He hung up the phone and took a deep, shuddering breath. The small comfort of having an appointment with his doctor didn't do much to quell the terror gnawing at the edges of his mind.

Chapter Three

Upon arriving at the clinic, Joseph was ushered into one of the cold, sterile examination rooms. Anxiety twisted his gut as he waited for Doctor Brown. When the door finally opened, the doctor walked in with a warm smile on his face, wearing a long white coat and a stethoscope looped over his narrow shoulders.

"Joseph, what seems to be the problem today?" Doctor Brown asked, his eyes flicking down to the towel wrapped around Joseph's wrist. His tone remained even and collected, as if it were just another day at the clinic.

"Doctor, I...I don't know what happened," Joseph stuttered, struggling to find the words to describe the nightmare he had inflicted upon himself. "I woke up this morning, and my right hand was...gone."

"Interesting," Doctor Brown murmured, his expression unreadable as he gently unwrapped the towel. The sight of the bloody stump didn't seem to faze him in the slightest. He had seen many similar injuries and he knew exactly what had happened to his patients missing hand. "Well, Joseph, it's not an uncommon occurrence these days. People are doing this to themselves more often than you'd think."

"Really?" Joseph asked incredulously, his eyes wide with shock and confusion.

"Indeed," Doctor Brown replied matter-of-factly. "Now, let's get you cleaned up and I'll prescribe some painkillers for that wrist of yours."

"Is that all you can offer me?" Joseph asked as the doctor began to clean and rebandage his wrist.

"What more can I do?" The doctor cocked an eyebrow at his patient. "You enjoy eating yourself, don't you? It tastes good, doesn't it?"

"Well, yes…I guess so," Joseph frowned back at the doctor, his confusion growing greater with each passing second. "But isn't it bad for me?"

"Everything in moderation," the doctor smiled reassuringly, as he began to wrap a fresh bandage about Joseph's throbbing wrist.

"Don't you think I need some kind of specialist?" Joseph asked.

The doctor shook his head and smiled. "The waiting list used to be at least two years long, but now, what with government cutbacks, your now looking at a five year wait."

"Five years!" Joseph exclaimed.

"And besides," the doctor continued, "You're case wouldn't be considered serious enough yet for me to even think about referring you to see a specialist. Maybe when you've eaten both your legs, come back and see me."

As the doctor went about his work, Joseph couldn't shake the feeling that something was terribly wrong—not just with himself, but with the world around him. And as he left the clinic with a fresh bandage and a prescription for painkillers, he couldn't help but wonder if anyone else shared his nightmarish compulsion, or if he was truly alone in his twisted hunger.

Joseph stumbled out of the doctor's office, his right wrist throbbing in time with his racing heartbeat. The fresh bandage covering the stump was thick and white, meticulously wrapped to staunch the bleeding. Despite Doctor Brown's careful handiwork, a few stray droplets of blood seeped through the pristine fabric, leaving dark crimson spots that seemed to pulsate menacingly.

Clutched in his left hand was a prescription for painkillers, the hastily scribbled words on the small piece of paper offering little comfort. Yet, it was as if the world continued to turn without a care for his suffering—an unsettling lack of concern permeating the air.

Chapter Four

"Hey," called out a voice, snapping Joseph from his daze.

A young woman stood nearby, her deep brown eyes filled with empathy. Her auburn hair cascaded down her shoulders, framing her pale face in soft waves. At first glance, she appeared entirely ordinary—that is, until Joseph noticed the empty space where her left hand and forearm should have been.

"Yeah?" he replied hesitantly, his voice cracking as he looked into her eyes. Something in them resonated within him—a shared darkness he couldn't quite put into words.

"I saw you in there with Doctor Brown," she said softly, her tone gentle yet tinged with a subtle note of urgency. "I wanted to tell you...I ate my arm and hand, too."

"What?" Joseph stammered, his eyes widening in shock. He felt a strange mix of relief and dread wash over him. Could this really be happening? Was he not alone in his grotesque compulsion?

"Look," she sighed, rolling up her sleeve to reveal a smooth, clean stump just above where her elbow had once been. "I know how you feel. It started with just a bite, but then...I couldn't stop. It was like my body was craving itself."

Joseph stood there, his mouth agape, as he tried to process her words. The thought of someone else sharing in his macabre affliction brought a twisted sense of camaraderie—a morbid bond forged through mutual suffering.

"Please," she implored, desperation creeping into her voice. "Promise me you won't let it consume you any further."

As Joseph stared at the young woman and his own bloodied bandage, he knew deep down that he wanted to resist the horrifying compulsion that had taken hold of him. But as his right wrist throbbed with pain, another part of him craved the taste of his own flesh, whispering dark temptations into the recesses of his mind.

The young woman looked around, her gaze darting from one passerby to another. Joseph followed her eyes, his heart pounding as he noticed as if for the very first time the missing fingers, limbs, and other body parts on those who walked by. It was as if a plague had descended upon the city.

"See?" she whispered, her voice trembling with fear. "It's not just us. So many people can't resist the taste of their own flesh...and it's killing them."

Joseph felt a coldness wash over him as he realised the extent of this horrifying phenomenon. What had once seemed like his own private nightmare was now exposed as a widespread affliction—a compulsion that was driving people to eat themselves, piece by piece, in search of a way to satisfy their macabre hunger.

"Is there no way to stop it?" he asked,

desperation creeping into his voice.

The young woman shook her head sadly. "I don't know. I've tried everything, but the cravings only get stronger. I'm terrified of what will happen when there's nothing left of myself to eat."

With a final, pleading glance, she turned and disappeared into the crowd, leaving Joseph alone with his thoughts. As he walked home, the faces of those he passed haunted him—each one a reflection of his own grim fate.

Chapter Five

That evening, Joseph sat in his dimly lit living room, the flickering light of the television his only company. He stared at the bloody stump at the end of his right arm, fighting back the urge to sink his teeth into the tender flesh of his forearm. Despite the pain, the temptation was overwhelming--a siren song that threatened to drag him under.

But he knew he couldn't give in. Not yet.

He forced himself to look away, picking up the remote with his left hand and flipping through channels until he landed on the news. The screen showed the Prime Minister standing in front of a shop window filled with prosthetic limbs and fake body parts, a reporter waiting to interview him.

"Prime Minister," the reporter began, her voice sharp and accusatory, "why are you promoting these fake body parts instead of encouraging people to stop eating themselves?"

The Prime Minister looked shocked at the question but quickly composed himself. "I would never tell people to stop doing something they enjoy," he replied smoothly, ignoring the reporter's incredulous expression.

"Isn't the cost to the Health Service spiralling out of control because of this behaviour?" she pressed.

"Again, it's not the government's place to dictate what people should or shouldn't eat," he said, then smiled into the camera.

"Are the rumours true that you have a financial interest in companies supplying these prosthetics?" the reporter pressed him. "Aren't you profiting from the fact that people are slowly eating themselves to death?"

"Look," the Prime Minister said firmly, his smile turning icy. "People eating themselves is their personal choice. They can stop at any time if they want to."

As the interview continued, Joseph found

himself unable to look away from the screen. The Prime Minister's words echoed in his mind, a twisted justification for the horror he knew was consuming him. It was true—he could stop. He could choose not to give in to his cravings.

But deep down, he knew that the taste was just too good to resist.

Joseph's gaze remained fixed on the television screen, his jaw slack as the Prime Minister continued providing evasive answers to the news reporter's pointed questions. He could feel the pain in his right arm throbbing, a constant reminder of the bloody stump that was once his hand.

"Personal choice," Joseph muttered under his breath, echoing the Prime Minister's words.

A part of him knew that he should be repulsed, disgusted by what he had done to himself. But instead, the taste of his own flesh haunted his thoughts, an insatiable craving gnawing at the edges of his mind.

The interview with the Prime Minister cut

to a commercial break and Joseph sat numbly and stared at the TV as he was bombarded with a string of glitzy and loud adverts, each one of them promoting sweet, flavoured sauces and spices to drizzle over one's arms and legs. *Eating yourself never tasted so good!* one advert claimed in bold neon writing accompanied by a catchy and unforgettable jingle.

Joseph glanced down at his left hand, fingers trembling slightly. The thought of sinking his teeth into them, tearing away the warm flesh and savouring the salty taste sent a shiver down his spine. It was wrong, he knew it, but the temptation was overpowering.

"I could stop if I wanted to..." he whispered, trying to convince himself that he still held some semblance of control over the compulsion.

But deep down, he knew that it had long since consumed him, dragging him further into a dark abyss of self-destruction.

As Joseph raised his left hand to his

mouth, the sight of his remaining fingers only fuelled the hunger that gnawed within him. He hesitated for a moment, his heart pounding in his chest, before clamping his teeth around two of his fingers with a sickening crunch.

The pain was immediate and intense, but it was overshadowed by the familiar taste that danced upon his tongue, flooding him with a perverse sense of satisfaction. Blood seeped between his clenched teeth, staining his lips and chin as he chewed on the severed digits.

"Too damn good," he groaned through ragged breaths, tears streaming down his face. A twisted smile spread across his bloodied lips, a grotesque mockery of the pleasure he found in his own self-destruction.

As the pain continued to throb in his mutilated hand, Joseph couldn't help but fixate on the Prime Minister's words once more. The idea that he could stop at any time, that it was all a matter of choice, seemed like a cruel joke.

But Joseph knew the truth—there was no

escaping the hunger that haunted him, no turning back from the path he had chosen. And as he sat in the dim glow of the television, his body forever marked by his own cravings, one thought echoed through his broken mind:

"Too damn good."

Sleep tight!

The Girl Who Was Struck By Lightning

For Nikki & Dave Fotheringham

Chapter One

The bell above the door jingled as another customer entered the Curiosity Shop which Dave and Nikki found themselves in. They gazed at each other over the top of the display that they were looking at, their eyes filled with a mixture of excitement and nerves that all new couples feel. Dave, a twenty-four-year-old man with unruly hair tucked beneath a faded baseball cap, wore jeans and a baggy t-shirt that had seen better days. A hint of a beard shadowed his strong jaw, giving him the air of a laid-back hippy.

Nikki, on the other hand, stood out in her long, flowing skirt and tie-dye t-shirt. A brightly colored headscarf adorned her head, and her wrists jangled with bracelets as she moved. Her bright blue eyes sparkled with mischief as she twirled a lock of her long, wavy hair around her finger.

"Dave, isn't this place amazing?" Nikki's voice was breathless with excitement, her cheeks flushed from the thrill of exploring the old town of Glastonbury and the old curiosity shop they had stumbled across. Dave couldn't help but smile at her enthusiasm, feeling his own heart race in response.

"Yeah, it's definitely...*interesting*," he replied, trying to match her energy. Despite their differences, there was a magnetic pull between them, a connection that had only grown stronger since they'd met at a local music festival a few months earlier.

"Look at this!" Nikki exclaimed, her fingers brushing against a small, dusty box tucked away on one of the shelves. She carefully opened it, revealing an array of colorful crystals nestled within. "Dave, these are incredible! Do you know anything about crystals?"

"Erm, not really," Dave admitted sheepishly, rubbing the back of his neck. "Why? Are they special or something?"

"Of course they are!" Nikki's face lit up as she began to explain, holding up a deep purple amethyst. "This is for protection and spiritual growth. And this one," she said, picking up a shimmering clear quartz, "amplifies energy and brings clarity. I've been collecting crystals for years. They have amazing healing properties."

Dave watched as Nikki's fingers danced over the crystals, her passion evident in her every word and gesture. He couldn't help but be drawn to her, despite his initial scepticism about such things.

"Okay, so how do they work? Do you just...hold them or something?" Dave asked, now genuinely curious.

"Sometimes, yes," Nikki answered, her eyes never leaving the stones. "But there are other ways to use them too. You can wear them, place them around your home, or even meditate with them. The key is to tap into their energy and allow it to flow through you."

"Like the force?" Dave smiled at her.

"Huh?" she looked up at him and frowned.

Seeing the confusion in her pretty eyes and guessing that Nikki wasn't a sci-fi fan like himself, he smiled and said, "It doesn't matter. Tell me more about the crystals."

As she spoke enthusiastically about the crystal holding some kind of mystic force, Dave felt a shiver run down his spine. The idea of tapping into some unseen energy seemed unsettling, yet he couldn't deny the allure of it all. Perhaps, he thought, there was more to this world than what met the eye. And if anyone could show him that hidden depth, it was Nikki.

"Alright," Dave said, reaching out to tentatively touch one of the crystals. "I'm willing to give it a try." His heart swelled as Nikki's face lit up with joy, her eyes shining with affection for him.

"Thank you, Dave," she whispered, leaning in to press a soft kiss to his cheek. "You won't regret it."

But little did Dave know that his journey

into the world of mysticism would soon take him down a dark and twisted path, forever altering the course of his life.

Chapter Two

The sun dipped below the horizon, casting long shadows across the street outside Nikki's small house where she and Dave were preparing for their upcoming adventure. It had taken a little convincing on her part to persuade Dave to join her on a trip to visit an ancient stone circle out in the country. But Nikki's enthusiasm for ancient sites was infectious, and although Dave had never shared her passion before, he found himself captivated by her stories of Stonehenge, the Pyramids, and other mystical destinations, so he had agreed to join Nikki on her trip.

"Did you know," she said excitedly, "that some people believe these stone circles I'm taking you to, were used for rituals and ceremonies thousands of years ago? They say that they're connected to powerful energies, ones that we can still tap into today if we know how."

Dave glanced at her, his eyes reflecting both curiosity and scepticism. "And you think we can do that?" he asked, a hint of disbelief in his voice.

"Absolutely," she replied, her confidence unwavering. "I've always felt a deep connection with the past, like I belonged to a time when people understood the true power of nature and the universe. It's why I love visiting these places so much. There's just something about them that calls to me."

Dave couldn't help but smile at her enthusiasm, even as his mind conjured images of shadowy figures conducting arcane rituals beneath a blood-red moon. As unnerving as those thoughts might be, he knew that this trip meant the world to Nikki, and he was determined to support her in any way he could.

So, together, they loaded their camping equipment into the back of Nikki's old camper van, making sure to pack extra blankets, food, and torches in case of an emergency. As he threw the last of the supplies into the van, Dave caught a glimpse of Nikki cradling a small velvet bag in her hands, her fingers tracing the intricate patterns embroidered on its surface.

"Those are crystals, right?" he asked. "You really think they hold some kind of magic?"

"Trust me," she said with a smile, her eyes filled with certainty. "Once we're there, you'll see just how incredible they can be."

With everything packed and ready, Nikki climbed into the driver's seat while Dave settled in beside her, a map spread out across his lap. The sun had all but disappeared by now, leaving only a faint orange glow on the horizon as they set off down the winding country roads. The air grew colder, and doubts began to cloud Dave's mind again as he glanced out of the window at the darkening sky.

"Are you sure about this?" he asked, over the rattling sound coming from the engine of Nikki's ancient camper van. "I don't like the look of those clouds. It looks like a storm is coming."

Nikki's gaze followed his, taking in the ominous mass of storm clouds that seemed to be gathering in the distance. For a moment, he saw a flicker of doubt cross her face, but it was quickly replaced with determination.

"It'll be fine," she assured him, her grip tightening on the steering wheel. "Besides, this is when the energies are strongest...just trust me, Dave. You won't regret it."

He nodded, trying to shake off the unease that threatened to consume him. Whatever lay ahead, he thought, they would face it together. And somehow, that knowledge made the encroaching darkness seem just a little less terrifying.

Chapter Three

The moon sat fat and round in the night sky, casting a blue glow over the landscape as Nikki and Dave navigated the narrow, winding road. Shadows flickered across their faces as they drove further into the wilderness. The atmosphere was charged with anticipation, and despite the growing darkness, Dave couldn't help but feel a spark of excitement. He stole a glance at Nikki, who was humming softly to herself in time with *Going Underground* by the Jam, which was playing on the radio.

"Tell me more about these stone circles," he said, turning down the radio, to better hear her. "What makes them so special?"

Nikki's face lit up, and she eagerly launched into an explanation. "Well, ancient cultures built these stone circles as sacred sites, places where they could connect with the earth's energy. They believed that by aligning the stones with celestial bodies, they could harness the power of the universe."

As she spoke, Dave found himself drawn into her passion for the subject. He had always been a sceptic when it came to matters of the supernatural, but there was something in Nikki's unwavering belief that made him want to understand—to share in the knowledge that she held so dear.

"Amazing," he murmured, his eyes fixed on her as she concentrated on the road ahead. "I never knew they were so important."

"Each circle has its own unique energy," Nikki continued, her voice barely above a whisper. "Some people claim to have experienced visions, healing, or even time travel while visiting them."

"Time travel?" Dave asked, raising an eyebrow in disbelief. Yet, he couldn't deny the thrill that ran through him at the thought.

"Maybe we'll find out for ourselves," Nikki teased, shooting him a sideways smile.

As they rounded a bend, the stone circle came into view, standing tall and imposing against the night sky. Nikki pulled the camper van to a stop, and for a moment, they sat in silence, awestruck by the grandeur of the ancient monument. The stones seemed to hum with energy, their surfaces glistening in the moonlight.

"Wow," Dave breathed, his scepticism momentarily forgotten as he took in the sight before him.

"Come on," Nikki urged, her eyes alight with excitement. "Let's go and explore."

With hearts pounding and adrenaline racing through their veins, Nikki and Dave climbed from the camper van and ventured forward into the unknown, drawn towards the stone circle that promised adventure, mystery, and perhaps something even more profound.

Chapter Four

The wind began to pick up as Dave and Nikki neared the stone circle. Dark storm clouds rolled in, casting an ominous shadow over the ancient stones. Dave glanced at Nikki, who seemed unfazed by the sudden change in weather, her eyes sparkling with excitement.

"Looks like we're in for a storm," Dave said, pulling his denim jacket tighter around him.

"Storms are powerful," Nikki shouted over the roar of the howling wind. "They can amplify the energy of these sacred sites."

Dave couldn't help but feel a growing sense of unease as they approached the stone circle. The air crackled with electricity, and he wondered if it was merely the impending storm or something more otherworldly.

"Are you sure about this?" Dave asked, trying to keep his voice steady despite his rising anxiety.

"Absolutely," Nikki beamed, her eyes locked on the stones. "This is what I've been searching for, Dave."

As they stood before the towering stones, the wind intensified, whipping their hair and clothes around them. A low rumble echoed through the air, causing the ground beneath their feet to tremble ever so slightly.

"Can you feel that?" Nikki shouted, her voice alive with exhilaration and her eyes wide with wonder.

"Feel what?" Dave yelled back, struggling to hear her above the roar of the storm.

"The energy!" Nikki cried. "It's pulsating through the stones!"

Dave squinted against the swirling darkness, his heart hammering in his chest. What were once static, silent stone monuments now appeared to vibrate and spin before his very eyes. An eerie, spiralling vortex formed within the circle, its ghostly tendrils reaching out towards them.

Is this really happening? Dave thought, panic flooding his mind. *Or am I going mad?*

"Come on!" Nikki urged, grabbing his hand, and pulling him towards the vortex. "Let's embrace the power of the storm!"

"Wait!" Dave shouted, his mind racing with a thousand questions and fears. But Nikki was relentless, her grip on him was like iron.

"Trust me, Dave," she insisted, her eyes alight with an intensity he'd never seen before. "This is our chance to truly connect with the ancient past."

He hesitated, his instincts screaming for him to run, but something in Nikki's unwavering confidence held him back. With a deep, shuddering breath, he took a step forward, his hand still clasped tightly in hers. As they entered the swirling vortex, Dave's world spun into darkness, his fear and awe merging into one terrifying, exhilarating experience.

The vortex suddenly dissipated, leaving Dave and Nikki standing in the center of the stone circle. The storm had calmed, but dark clouds still loomed overhead. Dave glanced around, his heart pounding as he tried to make sense of what had just happened.

"Did we...lose time?" he asked, noting the position of the sun hanging low in the sky. It had been night when they had stepped into the stone circle but now it seemed much closer to dusk as the sun was only beginning to set.

"Time is just an illusion, remember?" Nikki replied, her eyes sparkling with excitement. "Embrace the mystery, Dave."

As she spoke, she lovingly caressed one of the ancient stones, seemingly unfazed by the bizarre occurrences they'd just experienced. Dave couldn't help but notice that her touch left a faint, glowing imprint on the rough surface.

"Okay, but this is more than just embracing mystery," Dave said, trying to keep the rising panic in his voice at bay. "What if something dangerous is happening here?"

"Relax," Nikki said gently, looping her arm

through his. "We're perfectly safe. The stones have always been a source of power and protection."

Dave hesitated, torn between his concern for their safety and his desire to keep Nikki happy. He didn't want to be a killjoy, but the events that had unfolded so far were beyond anything he could have ever imagined—or even begin to explain.

"Maybe we should head back home," Dave finally suggested.

"Let's stay the night," Nikki said, her eyes pleading with him. "It'll be an adventure we'll never forget."

Dave swallowed hard, his mind racing. Part of him wanted to pack up and leave immediately, to return to the familiar comfort of their everyday lives. But he also longed to believe in the magic that Nikki so willingly embraced. And deep down, he knew that he would do anything to keep the spark in her eyes from fading.

"Alright," he conceded, trying to sound more confident than he felt. "Just for tonight."

"Perfect!" Nikki beamed, her excitement infectious despite Dave's lingering reservations. She squeezed his arm affectionately before releasing him and heading back towards the camper van.

As he watched her excitedly unpack their belongings, Dave couldn't help but feel a twinge of guilt for his doubts. He wanted to believe that the power of the stones was real and that nothing bad would come of their encounter with the vortex. But as the shadows grew long and night crept in again, unease continued to gnaw at the edges of his mind.

Chapter Five

Determined to put his worries aside, Dave reached for the tent poles and began to help Nikki assemble their makeshift home for the night. As they worked together, Dave's thoughts were momentarily occupied by the task at hand. He tried to focus on clicking the tent poles together and stretching the fabric taut over the frame.

"Dave, can you grab the pegs?" Nikki asked, her voice filled with laughter as she struggled to keep the tent from billowing out of control in the wind.

"Sure," he replied, rummaging through their gear until he found the small bag of metal stakes. Together, they secured the tent to the ground, their fingers brushing against each other as they did so.

With their sleeping quarters established, Dave turned his attention to gathering some more firewood as Nikki began to light the fire with the kindling, they had brought with them. Dave carried an axe to the edge of the nearby treeline and began to chop wood. The rhythmic sound of his axe biting into the wood provided a comforting distraction from his earlier unease. Each swing of the axe sent splinters flying into the air, as he struggled to control the inner turmoil that he felt.

"Hey, I think we have enough wood now," Nikki called out, admiring the growing pile of logs and branches. "Why don't you come and sit by the fire?"

Looking back over his shoulder at Nikki, he tossed the axe aside and joined her by the crackling flames. The warmth of the fire seeped into his bones, slowly easing away the tension that had settled there.

"Tell me more about your favourite crystal," Dave said, genuinely curious about Nikki's passion for the subject.

"Mmm, that's a tough one," she said

thoughtfully, her eyes sparkling in the firelight. "But if I had to choose just one, it would be amethyst. It's said to be a powerful and protective stone, and it's absolutely beautiful."

Dave smiled at her enthusiasm, feeling a sense of normalcy settle around them as the nearby fire took the chill from the air. They continued to chat and laugh, exchanging stories about their lives and dreams as the fire cast flickering shadows on their faces.

"Did I ever tell you about the time I accidentally dyed my hair blue?" Nikki asked, her laughter bubbling up like a melody that drove away Dave's lingering fears.

"No, but I'd love to hear it," he said, leaning closer to her. As she told him the tale of her hair dye mishap, Dave let himself be swept away by the magic of the moment—two people, sharing an evening around a campfire beneath a canopy of stars.

For now, the swirling vortex and the spinning stones were forgotten, replaced by the infectious sound of Nikki's laughter as she entertained him with funny and wild stories. And while fear still lurked in the corners of his mind, it was held at bay by the comforting presence of Nikki sitting beside him.

Chapter Six

A sudden gust of wind ripped through the campsite, tearing Dave from his sleep. His eyes shot open, and he realised that the fire had died down to embers, casting a weird glow across the darkened clearing. The night was heavy with electricity, the scent of rain hanging in the air.

"Nikki?" he stammered, reaching out to where she had been sleeping beside him. Panic surged through him when he found only a cold, empty space. "Nikki!" he called out again, more urgently this time, as he scrambled to his feet.

A storm was thrashing around him now, lightning streaking across the sky like jagged scars. Dave's heart pounded in his chest, his breath coming in shallow gasps as he searched frantically for Nikki. Torrents of rain began to pour down, soaking him to the bone as he stumbled through the underbrush, half-blind and desperate.

"Please, be okay," he whispered, a silent prayer to whatever forces might be listening. As if in answer, a flash of lightning illuminated the stone circle, revealing a sight that stole Dave's breath away and sent ice-cold dread racing through his veins.

There, in the centre of the circle, was Nikki—trapped within a writhing mass of vines that seemed to grow and coil around her with unnatural speed. Her face was twisted in pain and terror, her eyes wide and pleading as she strained against her captors.

"NIKKI!" Dave screamed, dashing recklessly towards the stone circle without a moments thought for his own safety.

His arms flailed wildly, attempting to tear the vines away from her, but each one he ripped free was instantly replaced by another. It felt as though they were alive, fighting back against his efforts with an unsettling intelligence.

"Dave...help me!" Nikki cried out over the howling wind. Her eyes locked onto his,

desperation shining in their dark depths.
"Please!"

"Come on! Come on!" he muttered, his hands raw and bloody from his struggle with the vines. They seemed impossibly strong, but Dave refused to give up. He couldn't—not when Nikki's life hung in the balance.

Turning, he darted back towards their camp, snatched up the axe, then turned and raced back towards the stone circle, which was now spinning at speed beneath the storm that raged overhead.

"Stay with me, Nikki! I've got you!" he shouted, trying to reassure her even as fear gnawed relentlessly at his own resolve.

As he swung the axe down, its razor sharp edge biting into the vines that encased Nikki, the storm raged around them, indifferent to their plight, and each passing second felt like an eternity as Dave fought against the relentless tide of nature's fury.

A brilliant flash of lightning seared the

sky, illuminating the stone circle in a stark, otherworldly glow. The earth trembled beneath Dave's feet as he frantically brought the axe down over and over again, desperate to free Nikki from her prison of vines.

"Almost there," Dave panted, his hands slick with his own blood and sweat. "Just hang on!" Nikki's eyes were wild, filled with terror, but she managed a weak nod.

"Dave...I can feel them...tightening...I don't know if I can..." Her voice was cut off by a sudden sob as the vines constricted around her throat, making it difficult for her to breathe.

"NO!" Dave snarled, hacking away at the vines with renewed desperation.

He could feel the storm intensifying, the air crackling with an electric charge that made every hair on his body stand on end. Time was running out.

"Please...hurry..." Nikki whispered between gasps, her face now bloated and contorted with pain. Dave's heart clenched with despair as he fought against the seemingly endless tangle of vines.

"Okay, just one more…" Dave began, but his words were swallowed by a deafening roar.

A bolt of lightning crashed down upon the stone circle, striking Nikki with a blinding explosion of light and heat. The sheer force of the impact sent Dave hurtling backwards, his body colliding with the damp earth as the axe went flying from his fist.

"NIKKI!" he screamed, struggling to regain his footing. His vision swam, the world around him a blur of darkness and rain-slicked stones. Staggering back towards the circle, his worst fears were realised as he stared with horror at the gruesome sight that now lay splashed before him.

Nikki's body lay scattered among the smoldering remains of the vines, her once bright and vibrant form now dismembered into bloody chunks of flesh that lay scattered across the stone circle in a shattered mess. Her limbs lay splayed at unnatural angles, blood pooling around her like a crimson halo. It looked like she had exploded. Dave's legs buckled beneath him, and he collapsed beside her, his hands trembling as they hovered above her ruined body, unable to touch her.

"God...no...please, not her..." his voice was a ragged whisper, choked by grief and disbelief as he looked down at his hands to see them stained crimson with her blood. "This can't be happening! This can't be real!"

Dave roared out in anguish as he touched his face to find it splattered with lumps of his girlfriend's flesh. He looked down at himself to see that just like his face and hands, his clothes and the nearby axe were also smothered with her grisly and gruesome remains.

The sharp wail of sirens suddenly pierced the air, jolting Dave from his nightmarish stupor. He looked up, his eyes wide with panic as he saw the flashing blue and red lights approaching. They couldn't find him like this—they would never believe him! No one would!

"Sir!" A police officer shouted, stomping through the mud towards him. "Step away from the body!"

"Please," Dave croaked, shaking his head in denial. "It wasn't me... I tried to save her..."

But even as he spoke the words, he knew how futile they were. The evidence was damning—it was all around him, on his clothes, on the axe and on his skin.

"Save it for the judge," the officer spat, roughly hauling Dave to his feet, and handcuffing him.

As he was led away from Nikki's grotesque and disrupted body, Dave's mind raced with confusion, guilt, and fear. How could everything have gone so horribly wrong?

Chapter Seven

Dave sat in his sterile prison cell, his hands trembling as he stared at the cold concrete floor. The weight of the conviction for the murder of Nikki bore down on him like a crushing boulder, suffocating his last remnants of hope. His thoughts were consumed by Nikki, her face forever etched in his mind as if it was still the very moment the lightning had struck.

"Visitation!" The guard's voice echoed down the corridor, snapping Dave out of his desolation. He numbly stood up and shuffled towards the small window in the cell door, expecting to see the familiar face of his lawyer.

Instead, an old woman with wrinkled skin and silver hair stood before him. Her eyes were a piercing blue and held a glimmer of recognition that made gooseflesh crawl up Dave's spine. Dressed in a flowing skirt and a tattered tie-dye t-shirt, she looked like a relic from a bygone era—but her gaze was unwavering and intense.

"Who...who are you?" Dave stammered, his heart pounding in his chest.

"Dave, it's me," the old woman replied gently. "Nikki."

"Impossible," he whispered, shaking his head in disbelief. Yet something about her mannerisms, the way she tilted her head when she spoke, made him question his sanity.

"Listen to me," she urged, her voice cracked and ancient. "When that vortex appeared, I lost time. I was transported back to 1744."

"1744?" Dave repeated, his confusion escalating. He racked his brain for some explanation, some rationalisation for this bizarre encounter. But even as he rejected her words, a strange sensation clawed at the back of his mind, whispering that she might be telling the truth.

"Dave, I know it's hard to believe, but I'm here now. I've lived an entire life...many lives...since then, but the last time I travelled back in time I ended up in 1965, so I had to find you…even if it meant waiting fifty-eight years to tell you what happened that night in the stone circle." Nikki's words tumbled out in wheezy gasps.

Dave stared at her, his thoughts spiralling into chaos. If this was really Nikki, then it would mean that everything he knew about the night she died—everything he had been convicted for—was a lie. And yet, how could he make anyone else believe such an improbable story?

"What do you mean you've lived many lives?" he asked, staring at her through his prison cell bars.

"Like I've already said, that first night…I went back in time to the year 1744 and I lived a whole other life," she began to explain, stooped forward, silver whisps of hair framing her wrinkled face as she stared up at him. "Then when I grew old and frail just like I am now, I went back to that stone circle on another stormy night and again I was struck by lightning and sent back in time...but this time to the year 1210. Each time I travel back in time I reappear as a twenty-two year old, just like I was that night I stepped into the stone circle with you, Dave. I've lost count of how many times I've travelled back in time, but the last time I was struck by lightning in the stone circle, I found myself in 1965. I knew that if I waited fifty-eight years, I would reach this point in time, so I could see you once again, Dave, and explain what happened to me that night."

"Please, Nikki," he begged, pressing his hands against the bars that separated them. "If what you say is true, you have to help me prove my innocence."

"Dave..." Nikki's gaze softened, and for a moment, he saw a glimmer of the young woman he had fallen in love with. "I'm sorry, I can't give you what you need. My journey travelling through time is not over."

Dave's heart pounded in his chest as the implications of Nikki's story hit him like a thunderbolt. The truth could set him free, clear his name, and change everything. He leaned closer to the bars, excitement bubbling up within him.

"Listen, there must be a way to prove it. A blood sample or something from the evidence that was gathered by the police at the stone circle...from the axe that they believed I chopped you up with," he pleaded through the bars at her. "The blood can confirm your identity!"

Nikki hesitated, her aged eyes flickering with uncertainty. She glanced past him and into his sterile cell, as if searching for an answer among the cold concrete walls.

"Even if we could prove who I am," she whispered, "it wouldn't change the fact that I'm not the same person anymore. I've lived many other lives, Dave, and there are still more places and times I need to visit. This is my chance to truly connect with the ancient past."

Her words stung him like a slap in the face. But it was what she said next that seemed to echo through the air like the tolling of a funeral bell.

"Dave, I can't stay and help you. Another storm is coming, and I have to head back to the stone circle," she said, staring at him through the cell bars. "I have to go…to go way back once more."

His heart clenched in his chest. The hope that had flowered in him moments ago now withered and died, replaced by a chilling despair. As he stared into Nikki's familiar yet foreign eyes, he realised that no matter how much he longed for her help, he couldn't force her to give it.

"Please," he begged, voice cracking with emotion. "They think I killed you…they think I cut you up with that axe. Everyone thinks I'm a monster! Don't leave me here."

"Goodbye, Dave." Her voice wavered, and with one last sorrowful glance through the bars at him, she turned away.

Dave watched her disappear down the

stone corridor, her once vibrant figure now bent and frail. The coldness of his cell settled over him like a shroud, and Dave felt the heavy chains of his incarceration tighten around him. All hope vanished with Nikki, leaving him with nothing but the crushing weight of a truth that seemed destined to remain buried.

As the door slammed shut behind her, Dave's gaze was drawn to the stormy sky visible through the narrow window in his cell wall. Nikki had been right, another storm was coming and with each flash of lightning, he couldn't help but think of that fateful night at the stone circle—the spinning stones, the swirling vortex, and the young woman he had loved and lost forever.

Sleep tight!

The Human Farm

For Lana Fotheringham

Chapter One

1,825 days in captivity

The fluorescent lighting flickered incessantly, casting a garish glow over the rows of cramped cages that lined the cattle shed of the alien-owned farm. Lana's cage was no exception. The cold metal bars pressed against her skin as she huddled in the small space provided to her, barely big enough to accommodate her emaciated frame. The stench of decay and excrement hung heavy in the air—an ever-present reminder of the horrors that took place in the vast shed that seemed to stretch away to the left and to the right without end.

Lana's long brown hair, once vibrant, now hung in tangled clumps around her gaunt face. Her green-hazel eyes, once full of hope, were now clouded with dread and despair. She spent most of her days lost in thought, trying to piece together the fragmented memories of her life before this hellish existence. All Lana could remember was that she had once been kept as a pet for an alien family, but when she'd reached the age of twelve, the alien family had no longer found her cute and cuddly so had brought her to the human farm.

As Lana shifted uncomfortably within her narrow cage, which was so small she couldn't even lie down and had to sleep standing up, her thoughts drifted towards an unanswered question that had been gnawing at her for years—the existence of male humans. Throughout her entire captivity at the farm and as a pet, she had never seen one. She had heard whispers and rumours, but nothing substantial enough to quell her curiosity. What happened to them? Why were they kept separate from the women?

"Psst," Lana hissed softly, attempting to catch the attention of the young woman in the cage beside her. "Have you ever seen a human

man before?"

The other woman, who appeared to be only a few years older than Lana, glanced nervously around before leaning closer to the bars separating their cages. "No," she whispered, her voice trembling with fear. "I've heard stories, but I don't know if they're true."

"Stories?" Lana probed, her heart pounding.

"Rumours say that the men are kept away from us for some sinister purpose," the young woman murmured, her eyes darting around as if the aliens could hear her every word. "They say that the aliens have some sort of plan for them, something dark and twisted. But I don't know any more than that."

Lana's mind reeled at the implications of this information. If it were true, it only served to further underscore the horrors that lurked within the depths of the farm. Even though the young woman's answer had been vague, what she had said had filled Lana with a sense of dread that settled like concrete in her gut.

"Thank you," she whispered, before retreating back into the recesses of her cage, her thoughts racing as the persistent flicker of fluorescent lighting continued its relentless assault on her senses.

What could be happening to the male humans? And more importantly, what did it mean for her own fate?

The unsettling nature of these questions left her feeling more vulnerable than ever, her mind spinning with the weight of her impending doom. As the darkness of despair threatened to consume her, Lana clung to the one thing that had kept her going all these years—dreams of a life of freedom beyond the walls of this nightmarish prison.

Chapter Two

2,190 days in captivity

Lana's heart pounded as she cautiously leaned towards the bars separating her cage from that of the young woman next to hers. The other young woman who she had befriended had been taken by the aliens and Lana had not seen or heard of her again—but that had happened over a year ago. A different young woman now occupied the cage next to hers.

"Hey," Lana whispered, over the hum of alien machinery in the distance. "I need to know something."

The young woman, her red hair dull and matted, blinked slowly at Lana, a mixture of curiosity and apprehension in her eyes.

"Have you ever seen or heard about male humans?" Lana asked. "Why have I never seen one here?"

The young woman hesitated for a moment, then leaned closer, her breath shallow and laboured. "They keep the men separate from us, until we're ready for breeding," she whispered, her eyes darting around nervously. "But we're not just kept separate until we're ready for breeding like we've been told all these years."

"Then why?" Lana pressed, her knuckles whitening as she gripped the cold bars between them. "What do they do to the men?"

"Rumours say…they use men…and us for food." The young woman's voice cracked under the weight of her words; her gaze unable to meet Lana's. "Both males and females are used for food. But the males... they're subjected to horrible experiments, torturous procedures meant to extract what the aliens can from their male bodies."

Lana's stomach churned violently at the revelation, her mind struggling to process the horrifying truth. She tried to silence the nauseating images that threatened to overwhelm her, but the gruesome reality was too powerful to ignore.

"How do you know this?" Lana stammered.

"Someone who escaped...well, almost," the young woman replied, shivering at the memory. "They were caught and dragged back, but not before telling us what they'd seen. The aliens take pleasure in our suffering. We're nothing more than livestock to them."

The young woman's words hung heavy in the air, as unbearable as the oppressive fluorescent lights that bathed their cages in a sickly glow. Lana's body trembled uncontrollably, her vision blurring as hot tears threatened to cascade down her cheeks.

"Is there no escape? No way to fight back?" Lana asked, desperation making her voice tremble.

"None that I know of," the young woman answered solemnly, a defeated acceptance in her eyes. "Not without risking unimaginable horrors and then certain death."

Lana closed her eyes, trying to block out the gruesome images that now haunted her thoughts. She knew what lay ahead for her—pain and suffering. And as she stood there, trapped within the confines of her cage, the horrifying reality of her existence settled like a shroud around her, suffocating any hope she might have once held onto.

"Eighteen..." Lana whispered to herself. "That's when they take us for breeding or...or..."

"Or slaughter," the young woman finished for her, her voice heavy with despair. "I'm sorry you had to find out this way."

Lana's chest tightened as she contemplated the implications of the horrifying revelation. When would she be eighteen? She had been brought to the farm aged twelve—how many years ago had that been. She had lost count of days, weeks, months, and years. All of them seemed irrelevant to her. But Lana feared that perhaps she had just a year left before the aliens decided whether she would be used for breeding of for food. Her hazel eyes met the young woman's gaze, searching for any glimmer of hope—any sign that there might be another way.

"Is there really nothing we can do?" Lana asked as she choked back tears.

"Every day I wonder the same thing," the young woman sighed, her expression clouded with despair. "But the truth is, I don't know. All I can do is try to prepare myself for what's coming."

Lana clenched her fists, feeling the cold metal bars biting into her palms. She imagined those same bars dripping with blood as the aliens carried out their sadistic acts of violence, mutilating and devouring her human flesh. Her stomach churned at the thought.

Chapter Three

Just like the first young woman Lana had befriended, the second had also been taken from her cage never to be seen or heard of again. The cage next to Lana's was now home to another young woman, with a shaven head and with some kind of identification tag pierced through the top of her right ear. Just like the other young women, this young woman spoke of the horrors that the aliens inflicted on human males.

"Have you...have you seen it happen?" Lana asked her, curiosity and dread building within her in equal measure.

"Once," the young woman replied, her voice hollow. "On the farm where I came from, I was sometimes let outside to graze in the open air but what I saw one night...well...it was enough to make me pray for my own death."

"Tell me," Lana hissed through her bars, not sure whether she really wanted to know but her own morbid curiosity getting the better of her.

"Are you sure you want to know?" the young woman asked, as if sensing Lana's inner conflict.

Lana nodded, her heart pounding in her chest. She needed to know what lay ahead, as terrifying as that knowledge might be.

"I saw a man...a male human," the young woman began, her eyes unfocused as she relived the memory. "They took him from his cage and dragged him to the centre of the farm. They tied him down, spread-eagle on a wooden table, and then they..." She hesitated, swallowing hard before continuing. "They cut into him with knives. They sliced off pieces of his flesh, his screams tore through the night. I watched them feast on his still-warm flesh, their mouths dripping with blood and gore."

As the gruesome scene unfolded in Lana's

mind, she felt her knees buckle beneath her. Her body shook uncontrollably, her breaths coming in ragged gasps. The thought of such unimaginable torture—the idea that she too could suffer such a fate—threatened to overwhelm her completely.

"Please," Lana murmured. "I don't want to die like that."

"None of us do," the young woman said softly, reaching out to grasp Lana's hand through the bars that separated them. "But until we find a way to fight back or escape, our lives will remain at the mercy of these monstrous creatures."

With the brutal reality of her future looming ever closer, Lana clung to the young woman's hand, seeking solace in their shared terror. Together, they faced the horrors that awaited them, their minds filled with violent imagery and dark thoughts that offered no reprieve from the nightmare they were living.

"Eighteen," Lana whispered once more, feeling the icy tendrils of fear wrap around her heart. And as the fluorescent lights above continued to bathe their cages in an eerie glow, she knew that her eighteenth birthday, whenever that might be, would mark the beginning of the end.

Lana's heart raced as her thoughts spiralled out of control. With each breath she took, the cold truth of her existence became a reality she could no longer ignore. Trembling, she leaned against the cage, feeling the cold metal bars on her forehead. She closed her eyes in a futile attempt to block out the reality around her, but the gruesome truth continued to claw at the edges of her mind.

"Make it stop," she whispered. Her body quivered with fear and anxiety, unable to find any ray of hope in the darkness behind her eyelids.

"Focus on something else," came the voice of the young woman next to her, her hushed tone barely masking her own terror.

"Like what?" Lana whimpered, feeling the

sting of tears on her cheeks as she tried to hold herself together.

"Anything," the young woman insisted. "Remember a happy memory."

But Lana had no happy memories that she could think of, even as a pet she had led a miserable existence, more often or not caged and only let out to be used as some kind of plaything to be teased and ridiculed. She had been separated from her mother soon after birth, so her mother's milk could be siphoned off for the aliens to drink. Lana had often wondered why the alien's gorged themselves on human milk when they were both two different species. It wasn't as if the female aliens didn't produce enough of their own milk.

Lana's legs gave way, and she sank to the floor of the cage, her back pressed against the unforgiving metal. With each passing moment, sleep seemed an impossible dream. She needed rest, but the thought of the horrors that awaited her put sleep out of reach.

"Come on," the young woman urged, her voice strained. "You need to rest. We have to be strong if we're going to survive this nightmare."

"Rest?" Lana spat bitterly, her voice cracking. "How can I rest knowing what awaits me on my eighteenth birthday? How can any of us sleep when our lives are nothing but pain and suffering?"

"Because we must," the young woman replied softly, her words laced with determination. "We need to hold onto whatever strength we have left."

Lana clenched her jaw, her hands forming fists at her sides. She knew the young woman was right—they had no choice but to find a way to endure this torture. As Lana squeezed her eyes shut, she forced herself to focus on the sound of her own breathing—in and out, in and out.

"Have you ever tried to escape?" Lana whispered to the young woman in the adjacent cage.

The young woman snorted bitterly. "What would be the point? Even if we managed to get out of these cages, we'd still be trapped on this godforsaken farm. Besides," she added, her voice dropping to a whisper, "I've heard stories of what they do to those who try to run. It's not worth the risk."

Lana shuddered, her mind conjuring gruesome images of mutilated bodies and blood-soaked soil. She knew the young woman was right—escape was nothing more than a cruel illusion—a fleeting fantasy.

Turning away from the young woman, Lana imagined herself outside the cage, running through fields of long, lush grass and wildflowers, her heart pounding with the exhilaration of freedom. But the fantasy crumbled as quickly as it had bloomed, replaced by visions of aliens tearing her limb from limb, their grotesque faces twisted into expressions of glee as they feasted on her flesh.

"Does it ever get easier?" Lana asked.

"Maybe," the young woman replied, a note of resignation in her voice. "Or maybe we just become numb to it all."

Lana hugged herself tightly, her long brown hair serving as a thin veil between her face and the surrounding horrors.

"Is there no hope for us?" she whispered, allowing herself one final plea for comfort.

"Hope," the young woman said, staring into the void beyond their cages, "is a dangerous thing to have here."

The young woman's words hung in the air like a death sentence, extinguishing the last flicker of hope within Lana's heart. As she retreated further into the darkness of her own thoughts, she knew that nothing could save her from the nightmare that awaited her on the farm—not hope, not escape, and certainly not sleep.

Chapter Four

2,555 days in captivity

Lana's skin had grown pale, stretched tight over the prominent bones of her emaciated frame. Her eyes, framed by dark circles that seemed etched into her gaunt face, were haunted and hollow. The constant confinement in the cramped cage had withered her muscles, leaving her legs weak and unsteady.

"Hey," the young woman called out to Lana, trying to snap her out of her spiralling despair. "We have to try to stay strong, okay?"

Lana raised her head just enough so she could peer at the young woman from beneath her bedraggled fringe. This young woman was a new arrival—the young woman with the shaven head and ear tag had been taken by the aliens six months ago—and just like the others, Lana had never seen or heard of her again.

"Strong?" Lana scoffed, bitterness lacing her voice. "What's the point? We're just...livestock to them."

The young woman leaned closer to the bars separating their cages, her eyes filled with a fierce determination. "Then we fight back," she whispered. "No matter what they do to us, we can't let them take our humanity."

Lana stared at the young woman who seemed different from the other young women who had once occupied her cage. This young woman seemed to be brimming with something akin to hope. But over the years Lana had learnt that hope was a fragile thing—easily crushed by the weight of her impending fate.

"Fight back?" Lana murmured, her hands trembling as she clutched at the cold metal bars. "How? I'm so weak, I can barely stand."

"Then we'll start small," the young woman said enthusiastically. "We'll find ways to resist, even if it's just in our own minds. We won't let them break us."

Lana closed her eyes, tears slipping past her lashes as she tried to picture herself standing tall and defiant against the alien captors. But the horrifying images from her nightmares—the dismemberment, the blood, the agony—all flooded back, drowning any shred of hope or courage she might manage to muster.

"I promise you," the young woman said firmly, "We'll stand together, and we'll fight until the very end. We won't go down without a fight."

Then as if to prove to the young woman and to Lana that trying to fight the aliens would be fruitless, two alien guards dragged a lifeless young woman across the cold concrete floor outside their cages. The dead woman's limbs were twisted at unnatural angles, and she left a trail of blood behind her. Lana pressed herself against the back of her cage, trying to avoid seeing the grisly sight, but the alien's cruel laughter echoed in her ears.

"Look at this pathetic specimen," one of the aliens sneered, its voice guttural and menacing. "She didn't last long, did she?"

Lana clenched her teeth, fighting back the bile that rose in her throat as she stared at the mutilated corpse. The dead woman's eyes, wide with terror, seemed to bore into her very soul, reminding Lana of the gruesome fate that awaited her when she turned eighteen. She couldn't help but envision her own body, broken and bloody, being dragged away just like the young woman.

"Please," Lana whispered, her voice barely audible over the sound of her pounding heart. "I don't want to die...not like that."

"Silence, human!" another guard snarled, striking her cage with a metal rod. The impact sent a shockwave of pain through Lana's already battered body, causing her to whimper in agony.

"Stop it!" yelled the feisty young woman from the neighbouring cage, her face contorted with rage and fear. "Leave her alone!"

"Ah, you still have some fight left in you," the alien chuckled darkly, its eyes narrowing.

"We shall see how long that lasts."

As the guards moved on, dragging their gruesome cargo behind them, Lana slumped against the bars of her cage, her body trembling uncontrollably. The sickening stench of blood filled her nostrils, making it difficult for her to breathe. She closed her eyes, desperately trying to focus her thoughts on anything other than the relentless horror that surrounded her.

"Are you okay?" the young woman asked, her voice soft and concerned.

"No," Lana admitted, tears streaming down her cheeks. "I can't take much more of this."

"We have to keep going," the young woman replied, her voice filled with determination. "We can't let them win."

Suddenly a gut-wrenching scream echoed through the brightly lit shed. Lana's heart raced as she imagined what new atrocity was being inflicted on her fellow captives. The thought that she could be next, that her body would soon be subjected to the same unspeakable torment, consumed her.

"Stay strong," the young woman urged, gripping the bars of her cage tightly. "We'll find a way out of this nightmare. We have to."

Lana nodded, though doubt gnawed at the edges of her mind. As hard as she tried to believe in their eventual escape, the overwhelming dread that enveloped her made it nearly impossible.

"Promise me something," Lana said, her voice trembling as she looked at the young woman through the cage bars. "If...if I don't make it, promise me you won't give up. Promise me you'll survive this hell and find a way to destroy these monsters."

"I promise," the young woman whispered, her eyes glistening with unshed tears. "And I want you to promise me the same."

"Alright," Lana agreed. "I promise."

As the two young women clung to the fragile promises, they had made to each other, screams continued to echo through the night—chilling reminders of the nightmare they were trapped in. And though Lana tried to focus on her newfound determination, the horrifying reality of her situation—the blood-soaked floor, the mutilated bodies, and the ever-present threat of unspeakable pain—remained a constant, inescapable companion.

Chapter Five

2,585 days in captivity

Lana woke with a start, her sleep disturbed by terrified screams echoing through the air. Her heart raced as she tried to make sense of her surroundings, the fluorescent lights above her cage casting sickly shadows over the miserable scene. She watched in horror as one of the aliens dragged a mutilated body across the floor, leaving a trail of dark, sticky blood.

"That's another one gone," whispered the young woman in the adjacent cage. "How much longer do you think we have?"

"I don't know," Lana replied, desperately trying to figure out what her exact age was in years. Had she reached her eighteenth year yet? "This nightmare never seems to end."

"I still say we should try to fight back," the young woman suggested in her usual feisty tone.

"We could use our chains to strangle them or something."

"Are you insane?" Lana hissed, her eyes widening in disbelief. "They're ten times stronger than us! They'd tear us apart limb from limb before we even had a chance to react."

"Then what do you suggest?" the young woman said, desperation now creeping into her voice for the first time.

"I don't know," Lana muttered helplessly.

As she spoke, the alien that had been dragging the body paused to look directly at Lana. Its cold, emotionless gaze seemed to bore into her very soul, filling her with an indescribable terror. In that moment, Lana knew that her time was running out—that soon, it would be her body being dragged lifelessly across the floor.

"Stay strong," the young woman urged, gripping the bars of her cage tightly. "We'll find a way out of this nightmare. We have to."

Lana nodded. As hard as she tried to

believe in their eventual escape, the overwhelming dread that enveloped her made it nearly impossible. With each passing day, the terror grew stronger, more suffocating— threatening to snuff out the last embers of hope that still burned within her.

Chapter Six

2,661 days in captivity

Lana's heart pounded beneath her sweat-soaked skin as she woke, the sound of her cage door creaking open echoing throughout the cattle shed. Her vision blurred and adjusted to the bright fluorescent lighting, revealing two aliens looming over her like twisted sculptures, their grotesque forms casting shadows against the bloodstained walls.

"Out!" one of them snarled, its voice guttural and harsh.

Before Lana had the chance to react or follow the aliens command, the creature's clawed hands gripped a thick rope, swiftly looping it around her neck. Panic surged through Lana's body, fuelling her desperation to escape the tightening noose. She gasped for air, feeling the coarse fibres digging into her skin, leaving angry welts in their wake.

"Please," Lana choked out, tears streaming down her face. "Don't do this."

"Out!" the other alien hissed, ignoring her pleas.

The alien farmers yanked Lana from the cage with brute force, causing her to cry out in pain and terror. She stumbled forward, legs trembling with every step as her bare feet slapped against the cold filthy floor.

"Get off me!" Lana screamed, clutching at the rope around her neck. She kicked and thrashed wildly, attempting to break free from the aliens' vice-like grip. But they only tightened their hold, dragging her along mercilessly.

"Shut up, human filth!" the first alien growled, its breath hot and putrid, like decomposing meat left to rot in the sun.

"Move!" the second alien barked, yanking the rope tighter still, choking off her air supply. Lana's vision swam, her lungs burning as she struggled to breathe. The world around her began to fade, replaced by an encroaching darkness.

Is this how it ends? she thought, her mind a whirlwind of fear and despair. *I can't let them win. I have to fight just like I promised I would.*

As her body convulsed in raw, primal terror, Lana's resolve strengthened with each agonising second. She refused to become just another victim of these monstrous beings.

"Keep moving!" the other alien shouted, its tone menacing and harsh.

Lana's heart pounded in her chest as the door to the shed swung open, and for the first time in what seemed like forever, Lana caught a glimpse of the outside world. Despite the horror of her circumstances, she couldn't help but be mesmerised by the sight.

The grass was an impossibly vibrant green, stretching out endlessly before her. Towering trees loomed overhead, their branches swaying gently in the breeze that rustled through their leaves. It was a stark contrast to the rancid cage she'd been imprisoned in, a place devoid of any life or colour.

"Move!" one of the aliens hissed, yanking the rope once more and jolting her back to reality. She stumbled forward, her bare feet sinking into the soft soil beneath them.

Stay focused, she reminded herself, her mind racing with thoughts of escape. *You have to keep your promise and find a way out.*

"I won't tell you again! Keep moving!" the first alien barked, shoving her forcefully through the doors of another nearby shed. The door slammed shut behind her, plunging her into a world of fear once more.

Remember the outside, Lana thought desperately, clinging to the image of the vibrant and lush landscape she'd glimpsed so briefly. *Remember what you're fighting for.*

The vast shed that Lana now found herself in was lit brightly, with concrete walls and a foul stench that hung heavy in the air. Lana's heart pounded in her chest as she was roughly shoved forward. The alien guards barked more orders, their guttural voices grating on her ears.

"Line up with the others!" one of them snarled, shoving her toward a group of young women her age, all standing against the wall with wide, terrified eyes.

"Please, no," Lana whispered to herself, her body trembling. She glanced at the other girls, each one looking just as desperate and terrified as she felt.

"Stand still!" another alien guard demanded, his voice laced with impatience and malice. Swallowing hard, Lana pressed her back against the cold concrete, feeling the terror pulse through her veins.

Is this how it ends? she thought, fighting the urge to cry out or beg for mercy. *I have to do something.*

"Begin!" one of the aliens commanded, and a guard armed with a rifle stepped forward from the shadows. His eyes were dead and emotionless as he raised the weapon, aiming it at the first girl in the line.

"Please don't..." the girl whimpered, tears streaming down her face.

The alien guard sneered before pulling the trigger. A deafening blast rang out, and her head exploded in a shower of blood and gore, splattering Lana, and the other girls with warm, sticky chunks of her brains.

God, no! Lana screamed inside, unable to look away as the guard moved methodically down the line, executing each girl with a single shot that sent brain matter and skull fragments flying across the shed. The smell of blood and death filled her nostrils, threatening to choke her as she struggled to breathe.

Think, Lana, think! she urged herself, her mind racing as the guard approached. *There has to be a way out of this.*

Lana's eyes widened in terror as the alien slaughtermen lumbered forward, their hideous forms casting an oppressive shadow over the carnage before them. Their grotesque, clawed hands reached for the limp, lifeless bodies of the young women, hoisting them up on chains that hung from the ceiling like nightmarish chandeliers. The naked bodies dangled upside down, their sightless eyes staring out at nothing, and blood dripped steadily from their shattered skulls.

"Tender meat," one of the slaughtermen grinned, gesturing to the corpses with a gnarled finger.

"It is," another agreed, his voice gruff and dripping with hunger.

They brandished their large knives, the blades reflecting the harsh light of the slaughterhouse, and Lana felt her stomach churn with revulsion.

With brutal efficiency, the alien farmers began to disembowel the dead women, their precise cuts slicing through tender flesh with sickening ease. Lana's breath hitched in her throat, bile rising as she watched entrails spill onto the floor in a gruesome cascade. She could only imagine the pain these poor souls had endured before their end, and now the desecration of their bodies seemed like a cruel mockery of their brief lives.

As the aliens continued to work, their knives tearing through skin and muscle, Lana struggled to control her rising panic. She knew that as long as she remained quiet and still, she might survive this horror. But the sight of the mutilated bodies, combined with the nauseating scent of death, threatened to shatter her fragile composure.

Please, let me live, she silently begged, her mind screaming for mercy that would never come. *Please.*

But the aliens showed no sign of relenting. The massacre continued, and Lana squeezed her eyes shut, willing herself not to cry out in terror. Yet despite her best efforts, a strangled scream tore itself from her lips, echoing through the slaughterhouse and drawing the attention of the nightmarish creatures.

"You next," the alien barked, his beady eyes fixed on Lana.

Chapter Seven

Final day in captivity

In the cold, blood-splattered slaughterhouse, Lana's breaths came in shallow gasps as she watched the alien farmers tear into their grisly work. Her chest felt tight, her mind racing with terror. But through the haze of fear, a spark of determination ignited within her. She would not allow herself to be butchered like the others.

"You next!" the alien barked once more; its eyes fixated on her.

The alien guard holding her prisoner, a monstrous creature with leathery skin and grotesque features, tightened its grip around the rope encircling her neck.

"Get off me, you bastard!" Lana screamed, adrenaline pumping through her veins as she seized her chance. With a swift, powerful yank, she pulled the rope from the alien's grasp. The suddenness of her actions caught her monstrous captor off-guard, causing it to stumble backward.

Run, for God's sake, run! Lana cried out to herself, bolting from the slaughterhouse as fast as her legs would carry her. The alien guards, momentarily stunned by her defiance, let out throaty roars before giving chase.

As Lana sprinted across the farm, sirens wailed around her, their ear-piercing screech heightening her panic. *I can't die here,* she thought desperately, her heart pounding in her chest like a drum. *I have to survive!*

The aliens shouted behind her, their voices filled with rage and hatred. They chased after her relentlessly, their heavy footfalls thudding against the ground and sending tremors through Lana's body.

Keep running! Lana urged herself, tears streaming down her face. *Don't look back!* But despite this warning to herself, a morbid curiosity compelled her to glance over her shoulder. The sight that met her eyes was one of pure horror. The alien pursuers were gaining on her, their blood-stained claws outstretched, and their mouths twisted into grotesque snarls. And behind them, the slaughterhouse loomed like a grim spectre, a monument to death and despair.

Please, let this be a nightmare, Lana prayed in desperation, her legs growing weak with terror. *Please, let me wake up...*

But the sirens continued to wail, and the aliens closed in, their monstrous forms casting long shadows over the terrified young woman. The grassy terrain beneath Lana's feet seemed to stretch on forever, each stride causing her to stumble and falter. Panic rose in her chest like bile as she attempted to put distance between herself and the hideous aliens that pursued her, their deep booming voices echoing through the air, filling Lana with dread.

"Come on, Lana, keep going!" she muttered under her laboured breaths, heart pounding against her ribcage as if threatening to burst free.

But then, disaster struck. The coarse rope that encircled her neck suddenly snagged around her ankles, ensnaring her in its grasp. She let out a strangled cry as she was yanked off her feet, tumbling headlong into the long grass.

"Fuck!" Lana cursed, thrashing about in an attempt to disentangle herself from the rope's relentless grip. The thorny blades of grass whipped at her face, leaving shallow cuts across her cheeks and forehead.

"Get up, get up!" she urged herself frantically, knowing that every moment wasted brought the aliens ever closer.

As she struggled, a sinister hissing sound emerged from within the tall grass, making her blood run cold. A thick, serpentine shape slithered into view, its scales glistening with venomous intent. Lana's eyes widened in terror as the snake reared up, its fangs bared and dripping with lethal poison.

"Please, no," she whispered, desperation

clawing at her throat as her pulse quickened. But her pleas fell on deaf ears—the snake lunged forward, sinking its teeth deep into her exposed ankle.

"Argh no!" Lana screamed, her voice raw and ragged.

Hot, searing pain radiated up her leg, setting her nerves alight as the venom infiltrated her veins. The world around her began to blur, nausea overtaking her as she fought the urge to succumb to unconsciousness.

"Can't... give up..." Lana's thoughts became fragmented, her body trembling with the effort to remain conscious. She knew that if she allowed herself to fail now, there would be no hope of escape—and the prospect of dying at the hands of these monstrous aliens was far too horrifying to contemplate.

Lana's vision seesawed as she gritted her teeth, attempting to push herself up from the damp earth. Her ankle throbbed violently, swelling grotesquely beneath the tight rope.

Each agonising heartbeat pumped more venom through her veins, further clouding her thoughts.

"Get up!" she hissed through clenched teeth, feeling her knees buckle beneath her as she tried to stand.

"The human is over here!" one of the aliens shouted, its voice a ferocious growl that sent tremors down Lana's spine. She could hear them crashing through the underbrush, their heavy footfalls drawing nearer by the second.

Can't...let them...catch me... Lana's thoughts were a chaotic jumble, her fear and pain threatening to overwhelm her completely. She willed herself to ignore the relentless ache in her leg and the dizziness that threatened to consume her.

"Stop!" an alien snarled.

Lana glanced over her shoulder, her heart sinking as she saw them closing in on her. The creatures were grotesque parodies of humanity, their hideous features twisted into expressions of rage.

"Please," Lana gasped, trying to back away, but her swollen ankle betrayed her, causing her to stumble and fall again.

"Pathetic human," the lead alien spat, yanking her up by the rope around her neck. Lana choked and coughed, her hands clawing at the rough fibres digging into her throat.

"Take her back to the slaughterhouse," another alien commanded coldly. They dragged her, kicking and struggling, through the tangled foliage.

"Let me go! Help!" Lana cried out, desperate for someone—*anyone* to hear her. But her screams were swallowed by the cruel laughter of the aliens.

As the slaughterhouse loomed in the distance, a dreadful sense of finality washed over Lana. She knew that once she was inside those blood-stained walls, there would be no escape. The thought of her life ending in such a gruesome manner only fuelled her determination to resist, despite the pain coursing through her body.

I can't die...not like this... she thought, her pulse pounding in her ears as she forced herself to remain present and focused on her surroundings. Every laboured breath felt like a small victory—each step closer to the slaughterhouse seemed to slow time itself.

"Into the shed," one of the aliens snarled, shoving her towards the open door.

"Please, don't do this," Lana begged, but her pleas were ignored.

As they dragged Lana back into the slaughterhouse, her heart raced, knowing that the end was near, but refusing to surrender to it just yet.

"Stand her against the wall," one of the aliens ordered, pointing to a spot beside the other unfortunate women. Lana's legs trembled as she leaned against the cold, blood-stained surface, feeling the terror radiating off those around her.

I can't let them know...about the venom,

Lana thought, gritting her teeth, and forcing herself to focus on her plan. She knew that if she revealed her secret, the aliens might find another victim to replace her, and she couldn't bear the thought of someone else suffering in her place.

"Ready!" an alien barked, prompting the others to load their rifles.

The sound of metal clicking into place sent shivers down Lana's spine, but she refused to show any sign of weakness. Her eyes darted from one executioner to another, taking in the cruel satisfaction etched on their grotesque faces.

"Please, don't shoot me," a young woman beside Lana sobbed, her voice trembling with fear.

"Silence!" the alien commander snarled, smashing his fist into the woman's face, causing blood to spurt from her broken nose. The woman whimpered, crumpling to the ground as her body convulsed in pain.

"Steady...steady..." Lana whispered to

herself, steeling her nerves for the inevitable outcome. She could feel the poison from the snake bite beginning to take effect, her heart pounding faster than ever before, and her vision blurring at the edges.

"Fire!" the commander roared, his voice echoing through the slaughterhouse like thunder.

The sound of gunfire filled Lana's ears, deafening her to anything else. In the split second before the bullet tore through her skull, she gave the aliens a defiant smile, knowing that even in death, she might still have the last laugh.

Idiots, Lana thought with grim satisfaction as her brains exploded against the wall. *You've just sealed your own fate.*

Chapter Eight

Day one of freedom

The alien slaughtermen descended upon Lana's lifeless body like vultures, their grotesque forms looming over her. Their gnarled hands grasped at the blood-slicked chains that hoisted her naked and mutilated corpse into the air, dangling her alongside the other unfortunate victims.

"Look at this one," one of the aliens sneered, pointing a taloned finger at Lana's shattered skull. "She had some fight in her, didn't she?"

"Too bad it wasn't enough," another alien cackled, brandishing a large, serrated knife. "Now she's just meat."

With brutal efficiency, they set to work on Lana's body, hacking off limbs and carving through flesh with sickening glee. The sound of tearing sinew and cracking bone echoed through the slaughterhouse, punctuated by the aliens' frenzied laughter.

"Her meat looks tender," one observed, holding up a severed arm and running a claw along the exposed muscles. "This will make a fine meal."

"Indeed," agreed another, sinking his teeth into a bloody chunk of flesh torn from Lana's thigh. "Delicious."

As the aliens continued to dismember Lana's corpse, they remained blissfully unaware of the deadly venom coursing through her bloodstream. They licked their lips and fingers clean of her blood, ingesting the toxin with every greedy mouthful.

"More!" an alien demanded, shoving a dripping slab of Lana's flesh into its maw, the poison seeping into its system.

"Save some for the others," a fellow slaughterman grumbled, slicing off another piece and greedily devouring it. Unbeknownst to them, Lana's sacrifice was becoming their undoing.

Days passed, and the venom spread throughout the alien population, silently and insidiously eroding their bodies and minds. They became sluggish, their skin erupting in gruesome sores and boils. Their once-sharp minds dulled, as confusion and paranoia crept in.

"Something's wrong," an alien commander hissed to a subordinate, clutching at his swollen and painful stomach. "There's a sickness among us."

"Is it...the human meat?" the subordinate stammered, fear seeping into his voice.

"Impossible!" the commander roared, slamming a fist onto a nearby table. "Our bodies can process anything. We are invincible!"

"Then what...what is happening to us?" the subordinate whimpered, watching as another alien collapsed to the ground, convulsions wracking its body.

"Find the source!" the commander

ordered, his own strength fading with each passing moment. "Or we will all perish..."

But it was too late. Lana's venomous gift had already sealed their fate. One by one, they succumbed to the toxin, their bodies breaking down from the inside out. As the last of the aliens drew its final, agonising breath, humans emerged from the shadows, reclaiming the Earth that had been stolen from them.

Lana's name would be remembered—her sacrifice etched into the annals of history. The girl who had refused to give in, even in the face of death, had become the saviour of humankind—just like she had once promised.

Sleep tight!

The Christmas Present

For Lynda

Chapter One

Colin's heart ached with a pang of longing as his thoughts drifted to his wife, Jenny, and their six year-old son, Fred. The life of a twenty-seven year-old traveling salesman was lonely at best, spent in dingy hotel rooms and on endless stretches of motorway—but his loneliness seemed even more pronounced as it was the day before Christmas Eve. Colin should have been on his way home by now, but his car had sprung a leak and the owner of the tiny garage that he had managed to get his car to, said it would take a few hours to fix. So, Colin couldn't wait to get home, not just in time for Christmas, but because he missed the warmth of Jenny's embrace, and the sound of Fred's laughter ringing through their small home as he grew ever more excited at the thought of Santa filling his stocking with presents.

As Colin meandered the narrow snow

covered streets of yet another forgettable town, he ran a hand through his short black hair and sighed deeply. He glanced at the time, knowing that he still had hours before he could collect his car, and he wanted to be on the road before the snow began to fall harder and he found himself trapped in this godforsaken town for the whole of Christmas. But this wasn't the only reason why Colin felt so glum.

Sales had been down this year—way down if he was being honest—and the money he had made from selling dishcloths and Tupperware had left a massive void in his bank account. In fact, it was more of an abyss than a void, and he hadn't even been able to afford a Christmas present for Jenny or Fred yet. When sales had been good over previous years, no matter where his sales trips had taken him, he always managed to find a little something for Jenny and Fred—a trinket, a toy, or something sweet for them to unwrap on Christmas day.

And as he continued to meander the

snowy streets, he imagined their faces lighting up as they unwrapped their Christmas presents from him this year. But there would be no presents this year. He was broke. So, with his hands thrust into his coat pockets for warmth, and with the chill wind blowing snow all around him, he continued to wander the small town, hoping he might find something—*anything*—that he could give to his beautiful wife and adorable son this Christmas.

As snow settled like a blanket over the roofs of the dilapidated buildings in the backwater town that Colin's sales trip had brought him to, he couldn't help but think it was a place that seemed almost forgotten by time. And as he walked the deserted streets, and despite the Christmas lights that twinkled in many of the shop windows, a shiver ran down his spine. Colin couldn't shake the feeling that the town was hiding something—something dark, twisted, and perhaps even evil.

"Looking for a gift, Sir?" a raspy voice cut

through the churning snow as if it was carried on the chill wind that almost seemed to claw and snatch at his coat.

Colin spun around, expecting to see whoever it was who had called out to him. But as he turned in the direction that the voice had come from, all he could see was a curiosity shop tucked away in the shadows. Its cracked and faded sign creaked in the wind as if beckoning him closer. Unlike the other shops with their sparkling lights and Christmas displays, this shop's windows were grimy, obscuring whatever lay within. But despite its creepy and unwelcoming appearance, it was like an unseen force was compelling him to step inside.

"It couldn't hurt to take a look," he muttered under his breath, convincing himself that it was just another harmless stop in his ongoing quest to find an affordable gift for Jenny and Fred.

So, crossing the cobbled street, he approached the odd and weird-looking curiosity shop.

Chapter Two

As he pushed open the door, a cloud of dust swirled around him. The air was thick with the scent of decay, making it difficult to breathe. The shelves lining the walls were covered in a layer of grime, laden with odd statues, books, and trinkets. Cobwebs hung from every corner, the spiders that had spun them long dead or hidden away in the shadows.

"Interesting place," Colin muttered under his breath, attempting to mask the sudden sense of unease he now felt.

"Many treasures lie within," a raspy voice replied, seemingly originating from nowhere and everywhere at once.

Stomping snow for his boots, Colin glanced around the dimly lit shop but couldn't see who it was that had spoken. And as his eyes darted around the shop, examining the bizarre items on display, a statue of a grotesque creature with too many limbs caught his attention, its beady eyes appearing to follow him as he moved through the narrow aisles. An ancient book bound in what appeared to be some kind of animal skin made his stomach churn, but he forced himself to continue searching as if he was driven on by some unseen force, even though a voice in his gut urged him to run from the shop and not look back.

"Jenny would love that," he thought as he spotted an intricate locket nestled amongst the oddities. Its silver surface was scratched and tarnished, but it had a certain charm that he knew his wife would appreciate. How much was it though, he wondered as it didn't have a price tag.

And what about Fred? he thought, I can't buy a Christmas present for one and not the other. Then as if by design more than mere chance, his gaze fell upon a small toy soldier, its paint chipped and faded from years of neglect. "Fred's always loved soldiers," he muttered to himself.

As Colin reached out for the toy, something in the air shifted. The oppressive atmosphere seemed to grow even heavier, weighing down on him like a crushing weight.

"What am I doing here?" he wondered out loud, his heart pounding in his chest. "I don't have any money. But more than that, this place doesn't feel right."

"Ah, I see you've found something," the raspy voice he thought he'd heard before, suddenly whispered from directly behind him. "A token of your love, perhaps?"

Colin spun around, but there was no one behind him, just the narrow aisles cluttered with the weird collection of trinkets and oddities. As his eyes scanned the shop for the owner of the voice, he was sure that he'd heard, Colin could feel beads of cold sweat dripping down his back as he clutched the gifts tightly in his fist. There was no denying it any longer—the shop was a place of darkness, and he needed to leave before it consumed him.

But despite every fibre in his body now screaming at him to leave, the dim glow of the curiosity shop's single flickering bulb seemed to have a hypnotic effect, and Colin simply shivered as he ventured further into its depths. As he continued to pass between the narrow and cramped aisles, he could see rows upon rows of grotesquely stuffed animals looming over him, their glassy eyes watching him as he made his way deeper and further into the strange curiosity shop.

"God," he whispered, taking in their distorted faces—the misshapen snout of a boar, the mangled fur of a wolf, its teeth bared in a permanent snarl. He recoiled as he brushed past a stuffed bear, its claws extended, darkened with age and grime. It was as if the creatures were reaching out from beyond the grave, determined to drag him with them into the abyss.

Colin swallowed hard, wiping his clammy palms on his coat. He couldn't shake the feeling

that something evil lingered in the shop—
taunting him, waiting for the perfect moment to
strike. His heart raced, tendrils of terror creeping
through his veins.

"Can I help you find something?" A voice
like splintering wood shattered the silence,
making Colin jump. He turned around, only to
come face to face with an ancient old woman
whose very presence seemed to sap the warmth
from the air.

Her hair hung in greasy, grey strands
down to her hunched back, and her crooked
fingers curled around a gnarled wooden cane.
Her eyes were sunken deep into her skull, like
pools of darkness that seemed to swallow him
whole. The skin of her face had long since
surrendered to gravity, sagging, and folding into
itself until it resembled nothing more than a
rotting corpse that had been left for too long
beneath the sun.

"Erm, yeah," Colin stammered, trying to
regain his composure. "I'm just, uh, looking for

Christmas presents for my wife and son."

"Is that so?" The shopkeeper leaned in closer, her breath reeking of decay. "You must care for them very much."

"Of course I do," Colin replied, unable to look away from the wrinkles etched into the old woman's face. "I love them more than anything in the world."

"Ah!" The shopkeeper's cackle seemed to reverberate through the entire store, filling the air with a sense of menace. "Such devotion is rare these days. So very rare indeed."

Colin swallowed hard, trying to ignore the bile that was rising in his throat as he struggled to maintain his composure. "Please," he whispered, over the pounding of his heart. "Can you just help me find a gift? But I should warn you, I don't have a lot of money. I wish I could afford more, but I can't."

"Very well," the old woman replied, her sunken eyes never leaving his. "But remember...be careful what you wish for. You may just get it."

The putrid stench of the shopkeeper's breath clawed at Colin's nostrils as she leaned in even closer, her wrinkled face mere inches from his own. Her eyes, milky and unfocused, seemed to peer into the very depths of his soul.

"Tell me," she rasped. "Do you love your wife and son for all eternity?"

Colin blinked, taken aback by the sudden shift in the old woman's tone. His heart hammered against his ribcage, threatening to burst free from its bony prison. What kind of question was that? It didn't make any sense.

"Erm…" he hesitated, searching for the right words amidst the swirling fog of fear now clouding his mind. "I…I guess I do, yeah. Of course, I love them."

"Ah, eternal love," the shopkeeper murmured, her cracked lips twisting into a grotesque mockery of a smile. "Such a beautiful concept, isn't it? But so very few truly understand what it means."

A shiver slithered down Colin's spine as he tried to comprehend the meaning behind the old woman's cryptic words. He couldn't shake the feeling that he was being led down a dark and treacherous path, but he couldn't bring himself to turn back now. He needed to find a gift for Jenny and Fred, and this strange, decrepit curiosity store was the only place in town that held any promise of something affordable.

"Look," he said, desperation seeping into his voice. "I don't know what you're getting at, but I just want to get something nice for Christmas for my family, okay? Can you help me or not?"

"Of course!" The shopkeeper's laughter echoed through the shop once more. "I have just the thing for a man who loves his family so deeply."

As Colin stared into the abyss of the old woman's gaze, he felt a cold dread settle in the pit of his stomach. He didn't know what she had planned, but he knew with absolute certainty that it was something far more terrifying than anything he could have ever imagined.

Chapter Three

With a guttural chuckle, the ancient shopkeeper reached behind her and produced a small brown bottle. The glass was fogged and worn, as if it had survived countless centuries of abuse. Her gnarled fingers traced around the cork, and she held it up for Colin to see.

"Here you are," she rasped. "A token of love that transcends time...the potion of eternal life."

Colin stared at the bottle, his mind racing with thoughts of decay and rot. The very idea of eternal life seemed grotesque and unnatural, like the twisted, mangled creatures that adorned the shop's walls. This can't be real, he thought, but the woman's gaze seemed to pierce straight through him, as though she could read his doubts.

"Surely, you're joking," Colin said, his

voice cracking under the weight of his disbelief. "You can't really expect me to believe that some dusty old bottle holds the key to immortality."

"Believe what you will," the shopkeeper replied, her voice a chilling blend of malice and glee. "But know that this gift is yours…for free…should you choose to accept it. A few drops, and your love for your family shall never fade."

The sickening stench of death hung heavy in the air, and Colin felt his guts twist into knots. He couldn't stand another moment in this hellish place, let alone entertain the thought of accepting such a monstrous offering. With a final glance at the bottle, he shook his head and began to back away from the counter.

"Thanks, but I think I'll pass," he muttered, his heart pounding. "This whole thing seems…wrong. You must be out of your mind."

"Very well," the old woman hissed, her cracked lips curling into a wicked smile. "Don't say I didn't offer you the chance to prove your love. And remember…eternity is a long time to live without them."

As Colin turned to leave the curiosity shop, he felt a sudden wave of despair wash over him.

"Wait!" the old woman's voice rasped, stopping Colin in his tracks.

He hesitated, his hand on the door handle, torn between the urge to flee and the gnawing curiosity that had begun to take root in his mind.

"Allow me to demonstrate," she continued, her ancient eyes gleaming with a feverish intensity. "Just a few drops of this elixir, and you will bear witness to the miracle of eternal life."

Colin turned back slowly, his gaze shifting from the shrivelled face of the shopkeeper to the small brown bottle she clutched in her bony fingers. The air seemed charged with an eerie energy as he took a few hesitant steps back towards her.

"Fine," he said, his voice a cracked whisper. "Show me."

The old woman cackled softly, the sound like nails on a chalkboard. She reached for a dusty glass jar containing a cockroach, its tiny body twisted and contorted in the throes of its final moments. With trembling fingers, she uncorked the bottle and allowed a single drop of the potion to fall onto the insect's corpse.

"Watch closely," she crooned, her eyes locked on Colin's face.

The seconds ticked by, and for a moment, nothing happened. But then, something within the cockroach began to stir. Its limbs twitched, its shell heaved, and before Colin's disbelieving eyes, it sprang back to life, scurrying around the confines of the jar with a frenzied desperation.

"My God..." Colin breathed, his heart thundering in his ears. "What have you done?"

"I've merely given the bug a taste of what could be yours," the old woman replied, her lips spreading into a knowing smile. "Imagine your wife, your son...ageless and unchanging...the three of you together for all eternity. And all it would take is a few drops of this."

Colin stared at the cockroach, now desperately trying to escape its glass prison, and felt an icy terror settle in the pit of his stomach. The old woman's words echoed in his mind—tempting and horrifying—but he couldn't tear his eyes away from the grotesque scene before him.

"Take the potion," she whispered, her voice laden with equal parts promise and threat. "A gift, from me to you. No charge, no strings attached. Just a small token of appreciation for a loving father and husband."

His disbelief and revulsion battled within him, but the image of his family—his beautiful Jenny and innocent Fred—swam before his eyes. His love for them was fierce, and the thought of losing them was unbearable. The old woman seemed to sense his turmoil, her smile growing wider as she held out the bottle, waiting for him to decide.

Chapter Four

Colin's fingers trembled as they closed around the small brown bottle. His mind swirled with conflicting emotions, teetering on the edge of sanity as he struggled to comprehend what he held in his hand. The old woman continued to smile, her cracked and ancient face watching him intently, as though she could see straight through him.

"Thank you," he muttered, his voice a hoarse whisper.

He slipped the bottle into his coat pocket, feeling the cold glass against his skin like an icy talon gripping his heart. He couldn't look at the old woman any longer—he couldn't bear the weight of that knowing gaze. Instead, he focused on the door, willing his legs to move, to carry him away from this nightmare.

The floorboards creaked beneath his feet, protesting his every step towards freedom, but

Colin ignored them. His mind was consumed by thoughts of Jenny and Fred, their faces swimming before him in an endless loop, urging him forward. He could almost hear their laughter, feel their warm embraces, and it fuelled him on, pushing him closer to the door.

As his hand closed around the doorknob, slick with sweat, Colin couldn't help but cast one last glance back at the shopkeeper. But she was gone—vanished as if she had never been there at all. Only the dust motes dancing in the air and the grotesque stuffed animals bore silent witness to their encounter.

A shiver of dread ran down Colin's spine, and he pulled the door open with a violent jerk. He stumbled out of the shop, gasping for air as if he had been drowning, only to find himself drowning once more in the swirling snow. Turning up the collar of his coat, he made his way back through the forgotten town in the direction of the garage where he hoped his car would now be fixed.

Guilt gnawed at his insides, tearing mercilessly at his conscience, but it was too late now. The deed was done, and the cold glass pressed against his hand within his pocket as he curled his fingers around it as if unable to let go.

By the time he reached the garage on the edge of town, the snow was falling thick and fast, threatening to become a blizzard. Wanting to get going before the roads became unpassable, Colin avoided small talk with the garage owner and paid for the repairs to his car on his already maxed-out credit card.

Without looking back—and hoping he would never have to come back to this town—Colin set off in the direction of home, icy flakes of snow seesawing down in the headlights of his car and smothering the town in a blanket of white, although Colin sensed that something dark lay hidden beneath its now sparkling and pristine surface.

The windscreen wipers squeaked and groaned as they fought to drive away the barrage of snow that bombarded Colin's car. He turned up the heat to max, but it did nothing to take away the chill that he now felt gripping his heart and clawing at his guts with ice cold fingers.

But as he drew closer to home, the sense of dread that he felt became less, and the memories of that old woman almost seemed to fade. But one thing Colin couldn't forget was the old glass bottle in his pocket, and the promise of eternal life for him and his family.

By the time Colin was drawing the car to a stop outside of his home, all feelings of dread that he had once felt had long since vanished. All he felt now was relief at being home in time for Christmas, and to spend it with his cherished family. It was as if he had completely forgotten about the sinister old woman and the even sinister bottle, she had given to him as a Christmas present for him and his family.

Chapter Five

The front door creaked open, and Colin stepped inside his humble home, weary from his long business trip. The scent of freshly baked mince pies and cinnamon welcomed him, the familiar scent of Christmas that instantly soothed him. As he glanced into the living room, he could see that Jenny had put up the Christmas tree in his absence, and it twinkled brightly with lights and strings of tinsel. Jenny stepped out of the kitchen and the warm embrace he shared with his wife was all he needed to feel at peace again. The sight of her golden hair cascading down her back, her blue eyes and the soft pout of her lips was all he needed to remind him of how lucky he was to have her. Their six-year-old son Fred, rushed into his father's arms with a delighted squeal.

"Welcome home, Daddy!"

"Hey there, little man! I missed you two so

much," Colin said, feeling the weight of the world lifting off his shoulders as he held his family close. It was on nights like these that made the days on the road worth it.

"Let's get dinner started, shall we?" Jenny suggested, pulling away from their embrace and leading him towards the kitchen.

"Sounds perfect," Colin smiled, taking off his coat and rolling up his sleeves in preparation to start chopping vegetables. He savoured moments like these, when the three of them could be together, cooking and sharing tales of what each of them had been doing while he had been away on the road.

As Colin began slicing through a pile of carrots, and Jenny told him how relieved she was that he had managed to make it home before the bad weather had truly set in, he suddenly realised his phone was missing. Panic surged through him, remembering the vital emails and contact numbers of the customers stored within it. He frantically patted down his pockets, searching for the device.

"Have you seen my phone, Jenny?" he asked, his voice a mix of anxiety and frustration.

"Did you check your coat?" she replied, concern etched across her beautiful face.

"Good idea!" He dashed out of the kitchen and into the hall where he had discarded his coat. Fumbling through the pockets, he finally felt the cold, smooth surface of the phone against his fingertips and relief washed over him. As he reached into his jacket pocket to put away his phone, he accidentally brushed his fingertips against the small glass bottle containing the potion given to him by the old shopkeeper. The mysterious liquid stared back at him, its dark appearance evoking a sense of unease, although he couldn't quite understand why.

"What have you got there?" Jenny asked, as her husband stepped back into the kitchen, his eyes fixated on the bottle that he was holding in his hand.

"Erm, nothing. Just something I picked up

on my trip," Colin replied, trying to dismiss it as an insignificant trinket.

"Interesting," Jenny said with a raised eyebrow, then without paying much further thought to it, she added, "Anyway, would you mind stirring the sauce for a moment while I put Fred to bed."

"Sure," he agreed, setting the bottle down on the countertop.

As he took over stirring the thick, bubbling tomato sauce, he couldn't help but glance back at the bottle. Its glass surface seemed to shimmer in the kitchen light, drawing him closer like a moth to a flame.

In a trance-like state, he found himself reaching out for the bottle and prising out the cork with his thumb. The scent that wafted out was intoxicating, filling his mind with inexplicable urges. His hand trembled as he held the bottle above the sauce, a few drops falling into the mixture below.

"Colin, are you okay?" Jenny asked,

noticing his furtive behavior as she stepped back into the kitchen.

"Yeah, I'm fine," he muttered, quickly replacing the cork, and hiding the bottle in his palm. He attempted to regain control of himself, shaking off the disorienting effects of the potion.

"Okay," she said hesitantly, turning her attention back to the pasta she was boiling.

As they continued cooking, Colin couldn't keep his mind off of the potion. He wondered what it would do, how it would affect them once they consumed the tainted meal before them. Dread began to twist in his stomach, but it was too late—the few drops he had added had already seeped into their meal.

"Bon appétit," Colin whispered to himself as he watched Jenny stir the pasta sauce.

"Why don't you go and kiss Fred goodnight, while I plate dinner up," Jenny suggested, blissfully unaware that her evening meal had been contaminated by the man she loved.

"Okay, sure thing," Colin smiled, stepping out of the kitchen, and heading upstairs to his son's bedroom.

As he pushed the door open, he could see that Fred was already asleep. Fred was lying on his back, the sound of gentle snoring escaping his lips. Colin moved silently towards his sleeping son, the bottle clutched in his trembling hand. He couldn't explain what was driving him to do what he was about to do. It was like an unseen force had taken control of his body.

"Please forgive me," Colin whispered, tears brimming in his eyes.

As he leaned over his son, the moonlight that cut like a silver blade through a gap in the curtains illuminated Fred's peaceful expression, unaware of the danger that loomed above him. With shaking hands, Colin tilted the bottle and let a few drops of the potion fall onto Fred's parted lips.

"Colin? Dinner's ready," Jenny's voice called softly from the kitchen.

Startled, Colin quickly hid the bottle in his pocket, guilt gnawing at his insides as he left his son's bedroom, closing the door behind him.

"I'm coming, my love," he replied, trying to force cheerfulness into his voice.

When he returned to the kitchen, Jenny looked up from her plate, concern etched on her delicate features.

"Are you sure everything's okay?" she asked, her fork hovering over the pasta.

"Of course," he lied, sinking into his chair.

"Okay," she said hesitantly, her eyes still searching his face for any sign of deceit.

Unable to bear her gaze any longer, Colin focused on his dinner, lifting a forkful of sauce-covered pasta to his lips. The moment the tainted food touched his tongue, he felt a foreign presence invade his mind, filling it with darkness.

Chapter Six

"Delicious," Colin said, forcing a smile.

Jenny hesitated a moment longer before taking her first bite, her instincts warning her that something was off, but she couldn't be sure of what. Shaking doubts from her mind, she forked some of the pasta into her mouth. As they sat and chewed their food, neither of them could now escape the dark web that had been spun around them, ensnaring their very souls in its grasp.

"Jenny," Colin whispered, feeling an overwhelming urge to confess what he had done.

But before he could utter another word, the first waves of agony began to wash over them. He looked at Jenny, and in her eyes, he saw the same fear that now gripped his heart.

"Colin...I don't feel...right," Jenny stammered, her breathing growing laboured.

"Neither do I," he admitted, his face

contorting with pain as they both sat there, trapped in the nightmarish consequences of his actions.

The potion was rapid and relentless as it burrowed into their bodies like a parasite, feasting on their sanity.

"Help me, Colin," Jenny whimpered as the full force of the potion began to feast upon them. Jenny's eyes widened in terror as an unbearable scratching sound invaded her ears. "Colin, do you hear that?" she choked out, her voice trembling with fear.

"What? I don't hear anything," Colin replied, his own suffering momentarily forgotten as he focused on the torment etched across his wife's face.

"Make it stop, please!" Jenny cried out, throwing down her fork and clutching her head in agony.

The insidious scratching sound that she could now hear intensified, drowning out all other sounds and shredding her sanity like a relentless swarm of insects burrowing into her brain.

"Jenny, I can't hear it. What's happening to you?" Colin asked frantically, watching helplessly as his wife began to jerk and convulse under the potion that was now consuming her.

"IT'S IN MY EARS! GET IT OUT!" she screamed, pushing her chair back from the table, and leaping to her feet.

Tears streamed down her pale face as her fingers desperately clawed at her ears, digging past flesh and cartilage in a futile attempt to silence the maddening noise. Blood gushed from her ears and down her neck like crimson rivers, splashing the white tiled floor that she was standing on.

"JENNY!" Colin shouted, reaching out to grab her bloodied hands, but recoiling in horror as he realised the extent of the damage she had inflicted upon herself. The gruesome sight was etched into his mind, a macabre sight he would never forget.

"Please, Colin...I can't take it anymore," Jenny begged him, her once clear blue eyes now clouded with pain and despair.

With one final, guttural scream, her body convulsed violently, and then went limp. Silence fell over the room as she dropped to the floor, blood dripping from her tattered ears.

"Jenny...no..." Colin whispered, over the sound of his racing heart.

Deep down he knew that he was responsible for this grotesque scene. He could see that the potion's malevolent power had claimed its first victim, and he knew Jenny wouldn't be the last.

Colin's heart hammered in his chest as he bolted out of the kitchen and raced up the stairs two at a time. He couldn't shake the image of Jenny's mutilated ears from his mind as he burst through Fred's bedroom door, dread coiling in his gut like a pit of serpents.

"Fred!" Colin gasped, his voice cracking with fear.

His six year-old son lay on the bed, tiny hands clawing at his ears, blood oozing between his fingers. Fred's eyes swam with tears, wide with pain and confusion as they met Colin's horrified gaze.

"Daddy...it hurts! Make it stop!" Fred cried out, his voice a strangled whimper. "The scratching sound...it hurts daddy...real bad."

"Fred, I'm so sorry," Colin choked out, his eyes stinging with hot, helpless tears. He rushed to his son's side, cradling Fred's head in his hands, which were quickly smeared with the blood streaming from his son's ears.

"Please, Daddy..." Fred whimpered, his small body shaking violently beneath Colin's trembling hands.

"God, what have I done?" Colin cried out, cradling his son's small body to his chest as his mind spun with sickening guilt at the realisation of what he had done.

The potion had poisoned them all, and he was responsible. His heart felt like it was being crushed within his chest—the weight of his murderous actions unbearable.

"Fred...I love you so much. I'm so sorry," Colin whispered, tears streaming down his face as he held his dying son close, powerless to save him.

Fred's once bright eyes began to glaze over, his frantic scratching at his ears slowing to weak, feeble movements. In one final, shuddering breath, the boy's body went limp in Colin's arms, his life extinguished like a snuffed-out candle.

"NO!" Colin screamed, grief-stricken and tormented by the knowledge that he had brought about this nightmare. His son and wife—the two people he cherished most in the world—now lay dead because of him.

"Forgive me," Colin sobbed, clutching Fred's lifeless body to his chest, the cold realisation that not only had the old woman deceived him, but she had also sealed their fates forever—for an eternity just like she had promised.

Chapter Seven

In the eerie silence that followed Fred's last breath, a faint scratching sound began to seep into Colin's consciousness—like nails on a chalkboard. The noise intensified, rattling in his skull until it was all he could hear. Panic and dread filled his veins as the horrifying realisation dawned upon him—the potion had not finished its work.

"NO!" Colin cried out over the deafening cacophony of scratching inside his head. Desperation took hold as he pressed his palms against his ears, trying in vain to block out the maddening noise. "Please...make it stop!"

The sound grew louder still, driving him to claw at his own ears with bloodied fingers. His nails dug deep into the tender flesh, carving rivulets of red as he sought relief from the unbearable sound of scratching.

"Jenny...Fred...I'm so sorry," he choked out

between ragged breaths, his vision blurred by tears and the agony of the unrelenting noise. "I didn't know...I didn't mean for this to happen."

Is this my punishment? Colin wondered, his thoughts a chaotic swirl of despair and guilt. Am I to suffer for what I've done?

His legs buckled beneath him, unable to support the weight of his anguish any longer. As he fell to his knees, blood streaming down his face from the self-inflicted wounds, the scratching echoed relentlessly within his mind. Colin screamed, although his voice was drowned out by the sinister noise inside his head.

"This is all my fault. I brought this upon us."

The world around him faded, swallowed up by the darkness of his own suffering. Consumed by the unbearable scratching in his ears, Colin's existence was reduced to a single, agonising moment in time. There, on the cold floor of his son's bedroom, he found himself trapped within the hellish nightmare he had unwittingly unleashed upon his family.

The scratching in Colin's ears intensified, growing louder and more unbearable with each passing second. He could feel the life seeping out of him as his screams turned to whimpers—blood raining from his ears and pooling on the floor beneath him.

"Please...make it stop," he sobbed, over the deafening sound of scratching.

But there was no reprieve—no relief from the relentless suffering he had brought upon himself and his family.

In one final, futile attempt to escape the noise, Colin clawed at his own throat, shredding the skin, and rupturing the veins beneath. As the world around him began to fade to black, the sound of scratching seemed to intensify, consuming his entire being.

"Jenny...Fred...forgive me," he gasped, red bubbles of blood bursting on his lips as his last breath escaped through his tattered vocal cords.

And then, silence.

Epilogue

Colin woke with a start, gasping for air as he found himself engulfed in complete darkness. The air was heavy and stale, the weight of the earth above pressing down upon him like a crushing vice. Panic surged through his veins as he realised the horrifying truth—he was buried alive.

"NO!" he screamed, his voice muffled by the confines of the wooden box that encased him. "Let me out! I didn't mean for this to happen!"

His hands shot up, fingernails digging into the rough wood of the coffin lid as he scratched and clawed with frantic desperation. Splinters pierced his fingertips, tearing through skin, then bone.

"Jenny! Fred! Can you hear me?" he cried out, his breath becoming shallower as the limited oxygen within his tomb rapidly depleted. "I'm so sorry...please, someone help me!"

But there was no answer at first, only the sound of scratching coming from the left and the right. And in the suffocating darkness he knew that his beautiful wife and son lay in graves on either side of him.

Then over the sound of his own fingernails scratching frantically at the underside of his coffin lid, he heard the muffled screams of Jenny and Fred.

"Let us out!" he heard them cry and beg from within their coffins. "We're not dead…we've been buried alive!"

The only response was the soft thud of dirt against the wooden lid, a cruel reminder of the fate he had suffered and the family he had destroyed.

As his thoughts became more frantic, the scratching sounds only grew louder as his wife and son tried to claw themselves free. As he lay in total darkness listening to the sound of his loved ones scratching at their coffin lids like wild animals, a sickening realisation dawned on him.

The old shopkeeper had promised him, his wife and son eternal life—but what she had given them was eternal torment.

An eternity of having to listen to his wife and son desperately scratching against the underside of their coffin lids—forever desperate to get out.

"Please," Colin whispered. "Please make it stop."

But he knew it never would.

Sleep tight!

More books by Tim O'Rourke

Kiera Hudson Series One
Vampire Shift (Kiera Hudson Series 1) Book 1
Vampire Wake (Kiera Hudson Series 1) Book 2
Vampire Hunt (Kiera Hudson Series 1) Book 3
Vampire Breed (Kiera Hudson Series 1) Book 4
Wolf House (Kiera Hudson Series 1) Book 5
Vampire Hollows (Kiera Hudson Series 1) Book 6
Kiera Hudson Series Two
Dead Flesh (Kiera Hudson Series 2) Book 1
Dead Night (Kiera Hudson Series 2) Book 2
Dead Angels (Kiera Hudson Series 2) Book 3
Dead Statues (Kiera Hudson Series 2) Book 4
Dead Seth (Kiera Hudson Series 2) Book 5
Dead Wolf (Kiera Hudson Series 2) Book 6
Dead Water (Kiera Hudson Series 2) Book 7
Dead Push (Kiera Hudson Series 2) Book 8
Dead Lost (Kiera Hudson Series 2) Book 9
Dead End (Kiera Hudson Series 2) Book 10
Kiera Hudson Series Three
*The Creeping Men (Kiera Hudson Series Three)
Book 1*
*The Lethal Infected (Kiera Hudson Series Three)
Book 2*
*The Adoring Artist (Kiera Hudson Series Three)
Book 3*

The Secret Identity (Kiera Hudson Series Three) Book 4

The White Wolf (Kiera Hudson Series Three) Book 5

The Origins of Cara (Kiera Hudson Series Three) Book 6

The Final Push (Kiera Hudson Series Three) Book 7

The Underground Switch (Kiera Hudson Series Three) Book 8

The Last Elder (Kiera Hudson Series Three) Book 9

Kiera Hudson Series Four

The Girl Who Travelled Backward (Book 1)

The Man Who Loved Sone (Book 2)

The Witch in the Mirror (Book 3)

Kiera Hudson & the Six Clicks

The Six Clicks (Book One)

The Kiera Hudson Prequels

The Kiera Hudson Prequels (Book One)

The Kiera Hudson Prequels (Book Two)

Kiera Hudson & Sammy Carter

Vampire Twin (Pushed Trilogy) Book 1

Vampire Chronicle (Pushed Trilogy) Book 2

The Alternate World of Kiera Hudson

Wolf Shift (Book 1)

After Dark (Book 2)

The Christmas Wish (Book 3)

Halloween Night (Book 4)

Shifter (Book 5)

Silent Night (Book 6)

Kiera Hudson: The Victorian Adventures

The Victorian Adventures (Part 1)

The Victorian Adventures (Part 2)

The Victorian Adventures (Part 3)

The Victorian Adventures (Part 4)

The Victorian Adventures (Part 5)

The Victorian Adventures (Part 6)

The Victorian Adventures (Part 7)

Kiera Hudson: Love, Blood & Vampires

Kiera Hudson 1988 (Part One)

Kiera Hudson 1988 (Part Two)

Werewolves of Shade

Werewolves of Shade (Part One)

Werewolves of Shade (Part Two)

Werewolves of Shade (Part Three)

Werewolves of Shade (Part Four)

Werewolves of Shade (Part Five)

Werewolves of Shade (Part Six)

Vampires of Maze

Vampires of Maze (Part One)

Vampires of Maze (Part Two)

Vampires of Maze (Part Three)

Vampires of Maze (Part Four)

Vampires of Maze (Part Five)

Vampires of Maze (Part Six)

Witches of Twisted Den

Witches of Twisted Den (Part One)

Witches of Twisted Den (Part Two)

Witches of Twisted Den (Part Three)
Witches of Twisted Den (Part Four)
Witches of Twisted Den (Part Five)
Witches of Twisted Den (Part Six)
Cowgirl & Creature
Cowgirl & Creature (Book One)
Cowgirl & Creature (Book Two)
Cowgirl & Creature (Book Three)
Cowgirl & Creature (Book Four)
Cowgirl & Creature (Book Five)
Cowgirl & Creature (Book Six)
Cowgirl & Creature (Book Seven)
Cowgirl & Creature (Book Eight)
The Mirror Realm (The Lacey Swift Series)
The Mirror Realm (Book One)
The Mirror Realm (Book Two)
The Mirror Realm (Book Three)
The Mirror Realm (Book Four)
Moon Trilogy
Moonlight (Moon Trilogy) Book 1
Moonbeam (Moon Trilogy) Book 2
Moonshine (Moon Trilogy) Book 3
The Clockwork Immortals
Stranger (Part One)
Stranger (Part Two)
Stranger (Part Three)
The Jack Seth Novellas
Hollow Pit (Book One)
Black Hill Farm (Books 1 & 2)

Black Hill Farm (Book 1)
Black Hill Farm: Andy's Diary (Book 2)
Sydney Hart Novels
Witch (A Sydney Hart Novel) Book 1
Yellow (A Sydney Hart Novel) Book 2
Raven (A Sydney Hart Novel (Book 3)
The Tessa Dark Trilogy
Stilts (Book 1)
Zip (Book 2)
Sink (Book 3)
The Mechanic
The Mechanic
The Dark Side of Nightfall Trilogy
The Dark Side of Nightfall (Book One)
The Dark Side of Nightfall (Book Two)
The Dark Side of Nightfall (Book Three)
Samantha Carter Series
Vampire Seeker (Book One)
Vampire Flappers (Book Two)
Vampire Watchmen (Book Three)
Vampire Knight (A Reimagining of Vampire Shift)
Vampire Knight
The Charley Shepard
Saving the Dead
Nightmares Before Bedtime
The Underground Ripper
Dead In The Basement
Dead Doll

Dead Hands
Toxic Snails
Chapel Girl
The Man Who Ate Himself To Death
The Girl Who Was Struck By Lightning
The Human Farm
Unscathed
Written by Tim O'Rourke & C.J. Pinard

Printed in Great Britain
by Amazon

32698011R00199